SK'LAR

CONQUERED WORLD: BOOK THIRTEEN

ELIN WYN

CLOCK
WALK
PUBLISHING

PHRYNE

The blaring alarm startled me so badly that I jumped. Scalding hot coffee splashed over the steel rim of my cup and onto the array of datapads on my desk.

"Shit," I muttered more out of frustration rather than fear. I'd woken up hours before my alarm was set to go off. I'd been doing that ever since our sky split open and genocidal bug aliens started pouring into our world.

That was over a year ago, yet I still couldn't manage to remember to turn off my alarm.

I grabbed a cloth and dabbed coffee off the surface of the datapads. I'd spent the better part of two hours reading over various reports from the city of Nyheim and nearly every surrounding settlement.

A little over a week ago, General Rouhr and Councilwoman Vidia – my boss- decided to make an ally of the giant tentacle-y plant-thing that had held us hostage not too long ago.

It turned out to be sentient enough to hold a conversation, which was a huge surprise to me. However, I hadn't had the opportunity to converse with it myself.

Honestly, I wasn't sure if I wanted to.

A week ago, I was brainstorming ideas on how to kill the damn thing. Vidia and Rouhr might've been able to switch gears and take their tea with the thing, but I wasn't ready to do that. After all, the plant-thing was smart enough to use advanced military tactics.

I should start calling it by its name, I supposed. The Puppet Master. Not sure who came up with that. It was clever when the thing was our enemy. It seemed a little rude now that the creature was our ally, but politeness wasn't one of my strong suits. I was too direct for that kind of thing.

I get results.

Sometimes I have to be kind of a dick to get those results, but I didn't lose any sleep over it.

The reports I'd been reading mostly consisted of various groups bitching about General Rouhr and Vidia's decision to accept the Puppet Master as an ally.

I could understand their hesitation. The average citizen wasn't privy to the details exchanged between their leader and the Puppet Master in that hole in the desert.

I, however, was privy to those details. In fact, I'd had that conversation, and all others following, carefully transcribed and sent to me. That was what was on one of the many datapads strewn across my workspace.

Once the spilled coffee was wiped up, I got up to get ready for my day. I'd gotten a fair amount of work done, but nowhere near as much as I'd wanted to have done by now.

Vidia often said that was one of my downfalls. I could do ten times the work of everyone else and still think I hadn't done enough.

I walked to my bathroom. My apartment complex was right next to the central government building in Nyheim. It came complimentary with the job.

Damn good thing it did, too. My home was destroyed during the Xathi invasion.

I knew that didn't make me special.

Plenty of other people lost so much more than just their home. In fact, my apartment was so nice in comparison to all of the emergency housing that I often felt guilty.

Whole families were crammed into an apartment

the size of a shoebox. Here I was, in my studio with my bathroom that bordered on luxurious in comparison to others.

Three people could fit in my shower. I consistently had hot water, a luxury many often went without.

As guilty as I felt for having things so many didn't, I knew I'd earned these rewards. Even before aliens invaded my world, I had worked hard, harder than anyone. It took years for me to get where I was now.

My first job after leaving the orphanage where I spent my childhood was as an assistant to the security department in Fraga.

Now I *was* the security department.

Everything went through me, at least where the humans were concerned. I didn't have authority over General Rouhr's aliens. That was something that irked me but was simultaneously a relief.

Over the past few months, I'd gotten plenty of opportunities to work with the Skotan, K'ver, and Valorni soldiers. They were far more advanced than any human soldier could ever hope to be. They had better weapons and first-rate training.

However, even the mildest of our alien allies had an element of unpredictability that would not be fun to try to control. I didn't envy General Rouhr when it came to that aspect of his job. No wonder he always looked somewhat disgruntled.

As I scrubbed my hair and skin with a bar of standard-issue soap that smelled like wax, I went over what I had to get done today.

Vidia wanted to do a press conference of some kind soon. I didn't think it was a good idea, not yet.

Things were still too volatile among the people. As of right now, the aliens were tolerated by their respective communities. Some people welcomed them with open arms. Some people were practically frothing at the mouth to expel all aliens from the planet.

Vidia wasn't overly concerned with those people. She believed the anti-alien factions to be very small and spread out.

However, based on reports I'd been reading over the last two days, I had reason to suspect the anti-alien mindset was more widespread than Vidia thought.

Then there was the matter of the Puppet Master. How was I supposed to work something like that creature into my security protocols? It's not like I could fingerprint it and have it scanned into the systems. Naturally, the Puppet Master's strengths would be in the defense department. Or as a spy. It still amazed me that something so big had stayed hidden for so long.

My water pressure flickered, jarring me out of my thoughts. I'd been in the shower for too long. I was going to fall behind if I didn't pick up the pace.

I stepped out of the shower, dried off, and pulled on

my work clothes for the day. Technically, I didn't have a uniform, but I wore the same dark, close-fitting pants and the same tactical shirt in different colors most days.

Today, I chose a thunder-cloud-gray shirt.

Before I left my apartment, I caught a glimpse of myself in the mirror.

My chin length red hair was still wet. Hopefully, it would dry nicely. I didn't spend hours primping in front of a mirror, but that didn't mean I wanted to look like a ragamuffin.

Lack of sleep had made my complexion look a little wan as of late, but only I would notice something like that about myself. Light bounced off my sharp cheekbones, making me look more angular than I really was.

I always thought my blue eyes were a little too big for my face, but that came in handy when I wanted to shoot someone down with a withering stare.

Overall, I looked fine enough for work.

The walk to the central building was quick. I hadn't made it to the elevators before two human males stepped up to me.

"Good morning, ma'am," the first said.

"Is there anything we should know for the briefing today?" the second asked.

I gave them a blank look.

"Are you trainees?" I asked.

"No," the first said slowly. The second tried to subtly roll his eyes, but I caught the movement. "I'm Tona. This is Skit."

They said it like their names should mean something to me.

"We've met several times."

"I meet people every day," I replied.

"General Rouhr assigned us to your team yesterday because of our work with the hybrid outbreak?" The other one, Skit, prompted.

"Oh." A tight smile spread across my lips. "I remember now. I wouldn't have thought I'd forget the two guards injected into my squad without my approval or even my permission."

My squad was hand selected to my specifications. It had taken the better part of a year to assemble my elite team. I was very selective. The interview process was extremely thorough.

"With all due respect, ma'am, we're more than just a pair of frontier guards. We wouldn't be here if General Rouhr didn't think we deserved it," Tona said.

"Be that as it may," I pressed, "General Rouhr isn't your boss. You're on my squad now, which makes me your boss. The only thing that matters now is that you do your job to my standards, not General Rouhr's. Are we understood?"

Tona and Skit saluted to show their understanding.

"Good boys."

I moved past them and entered the elevator. The doors closed before the two of them could step onto the car. I relished the final moments of silence before my work day truly began. There was a briefing in a few hours.

I still had a few details I wanted to smooth over.

I was planning on bringing up the anti-alien factions. New construction projects were popping up all over the settled land. Each project would need its own security detail.

We'd already learned that anti-alien radicals had no issue disrupting construction projects.

That little nugget of logic was lost on me.

Why target efforts that would make life better for fellow humans?

Some of General Rouhr's best soldiers were scheduled to be in the briefing today. Some of them spent a lot of time in the field lately.

Perhaps they would offer insight into the behavior of the anti-alien groups. Assuming any of the radicals were ballsy enough to openly harass a group of General Rouhr's soldiers, that is.

The anti-alien radicals we'd interacted with thus far were that ballsy, but also very stupid. It stood to reason that future factions would be less foolhardy, especially since we were cracking down with punishments.

Whatever the case, this briefing was sure to be an interesting one.

SK'LAR

The cargo ship's engines hummed merrily as we gained altitude in the clear blue sky. From my position in the cockpit of the atmosphere-bound ship, I could see the uneven skyline of Amarita spread out in the distance on the shores of the crawling sea.

"Approaching Amarita proper on vector 201x."

I turned to regard the corporal piloting our craft. He was a K'ver, just as I was. Jet black skin rippled with muscle in his toned forearms, emblazoned with hair-thin silver circuitry. Since he was low in rank, he only had the most basic implants.

As a ranking officer, I had many more. For example, an implant near the back of my brain increased the flow of neurons between my nervous and muscular systems, meaning I could stand steady, even when our craft encountered the stiff wind blowing off the coast.

"Minor turbulence, sir. Compensating."

"Hold her steady, Corporal. The last thing we need is to crash on top of a human dwelling and stir up more xenophobia."

"Yes, sir." The corporal's hands flashed over the controls, and soon the chassis stopped shaking. He glanced at me, black eyes inscrutable. "Sir, if I may ask a question?"

"I believe you just did, Corporal, but go ahead."

"Yes, sir. Hasn't the anti-alien sentiment mostly run its course by now? I mean, after the whole mind-wiping fiasco?"

"You keep a close eye on current events, I see." I nodded in approval. "Yes, their movement has definitely taken a hit, and many humans have rejected them. However, if there's one thing that my admittedly shallow perusal of human history tells me, many of their species don't behave rationally. There was one orange-skinned fellow in the early twenty-first century who—"

A light flashed on the console, and the Corporal quickly scanned a read out.

"Report?"

"Sir, sensors are picking up some sort of structures

near the *Vengeance* crater. It looks like the start of a settlement or colony."

I pressed my lips together, considering options. I walked over to sit down at one of the monitoring stations.

"Patch in the feed to my screen, Corporal."

"Yes, sir."

The monitor flashed briefly, then depicted a series of crudely constructed buildings surrounded by a perimeter fence. I held my chin in my hand as I took in the sight of some salvaged atmospheric transports which had been modified with weaponry.

The compound seemed to be abuzz with activity, and I quickly lost count of how many bodies were milling about in the throng.

"Corporal, get me an estimate on the number of life signs within that compound."

"Yes, sir." His fingers whizzed across the console, making adjustments even as he continued to keep our flight steady. "It appears that I can't give you an accurate estimate. The compound has jamming technology. I can only scan those life forms outside of its walls."

I already knew the answer before I asked my next question, but I had to verify my intuition.

"What's the racial breakdown of the life forms you can scan, Corporal?"

He fiddled with the console for a bit, then turned his head around to regard me with a grim expression.

"All human, sir."

"I see." Silently observing the compound as I pondered what our next move should be, I felt a certain trepidation building within me. These were the kinds of decisions I was supposed to make as a Team Commander.

But I couldn't help but feel like I was out of my element. I knew I was a capable soldier, and my implants put me in the league of the other species. I couldn't arm-wrestle a Valorni, perhaps, but I would bet on myself in a fist fight, none the less.

However, I had limited experience with command positions. In many ways, I wondered if I wasn't appointed the head of Team Three just because of convenience, and not because I was the best candidate for the job.

Here I stood, for good or ill, and the corporal was waiting for me to make a decision. We should just finish the supply run, but the compound hadn't been on any briefings that had been disclosed to me. I couldn't pass up the opportunity to garner new information on what could be a potential threat to peace.

"Take us down, Corporal."

"Sir?" He couldn't quite hide a note of fear in his

tone. I couldn't blame him. The last thing I wanted to do was land in a nest of hostile humans.

The potential gains outweighed the risks, though.

"You have your orders."

"Understood, sir."

"But try to bring us down near the southern gate. Most of their vehicles and munitions seem to be concentrated to the northeast. If they want to get... testy...we'll be in a good position to retreat."

"Yes, sir."

The corporal took us into a shallow dive into the blasted, melted-rock crater where the *Vengeance* once stood. Now there was nothing left but scraps and a crater where that mighty vessel had rested, and if that was not a warning to be cautious, I didn't know what was.

We dipped down below the level of the compound. Multicolored strata flashed past the viewport as we skimmed just beneath the lip of the crater.

I doubted they had any weaponry trained on the crater itself, but apprehension still threatened to overwhelm me. At any moment, our unshielded, peaceful vessel might be perforated by fire from hostile humans.

I knew I shouldn't make assumptions. Just because this was an unregistered settlement of purely humans didn't automatically make them hostile.

But I had learned as a warrior that it was not just your brain that you must rely on, but your instinct. The humans called it 'going with your gut', which was about as silly a notion as I could imagine, but now, in the moment, I believed I was beginning to understand its meaning.

The corporal nosed the ship up and we flashed above the crater's edge. It was obvious that our arrival had not gone unnoticed. A large group of humans were clustered about the southern gate, and even from this distance, they didn't seem all that friendly.

"I guess this is the Welcome Wagon."

"Sir?" The corporal's brow wrinkled in confusion.

"It's a human expression. I was being sarcastic. I think we'd best prepare for antagonism from these creatures."

"Agreed."

The corporal set our craft down about thirty yards away from the gate. Our landing pylons had barely extended onto the grassy turf when the gate opened and the mob of humanity came spilling out.

They weren't charging our position, but they walked with a menacing purpose that made me second-guess my decision to investigate.

"Keep her hot and ready to lift off," I clapped my hand on his shoulder. My old CO used to do that, and oddly, it helped calm my nerves.

"Yes, sir."

My boots clanked off the metal deck plating as I went down into the cargo bay. Because this was a peaceful supply run, I didn't have the entirety of Team Three with me. However, protocol insisted that I bring at least three along, even on an ostensibly peaceful mission.

The biggest member of my crew was Tyehn. A big, burly Valorni, he had to cut the sleeves off his skinsuit to accommodate his size.

I silently considered if I should speak to someone about him; I swore he kept getting bigger each time I saw him. Tyehn held his salute crisply, perhaps because his laughter had been the most boisterous when I came below deck.

Jalok stood two inches shorter than Tyehn, but one look at his stone-cold expression and you realized that he was the one you should be afraid of.

Jalok was an expert at close-quarter combat, though he was pretty accurate with munitions as well, and those Skotan scales were a helpful defense.

Finally, Cazak gave me his version of a salute, which was limp and casual. He wasn't the most intimidating being in a fight, but he had a true knack for maintaining and repairing field equipment. Cazak was the only member of my team I had requested by name, but to be honest, it hadn't been hard to get him. His attitude rubbed a lot of commanders the wrong way, to use a human phrase.

"At ease." They relaxed somewhat, and Cazak gave me a little smirk I chose to ignore, even though it hit me right in my confidence. "As I'm sure you've noticed, we've made an unscheduled landing. There's a human settlement that's not supposed to be here, and we are going to make contact."

"Finally, some action." Tyehn reached for a two-handed pulse rifle, but I held up my hand and shook my head.

"Not so fast. You're a bit too threatening in appearance. Head up front and assist our pilot in any way he wishes."

His face crinkled with disappointment.

"But he's only a corporal."

"In any way he wishes, Tyehn."

"Yes, sir."

With a sigh of resignation, he headed up to the front. I turned my attention to the other two.

"Small sidearms only. We don't want to alarm them."

With Jalok and Cazak in tow, I pressed the panel which lowered the exit ramp. The crowd of humans had gathered a short distance away. When they first caught sight of us in our skinsuits, they started booing.

Jalok tensed up next to me. I whispered surreptitiously in his ear.

"Easy, Jalok. We're not here to fight."

"Try telling that to *them*." Still, his fingers uncurled from around the grip of his side-arm.

I approached the throng with purpose, refusing to show any sign of weakness while still trying to appear non-threatening.

An older human male stepped forward, a slapdash projectile weapon clutched in one hand. At least the barrels were pointed at the ground—for now.

"Salutations." I offered a small bow of my head, and my soldiers followed suit. "I am Commander Sk'lar of the K'ver Central Command," a small lie. "Who speaks for you?"

In response, one of the humans spat a wad of white froth at my feet. Jalok's eyes narrowed, but he held his place.

The older human grinned at the display and stepped right up in front of me.

"I speak for us. And if you can't tell, you obsidian-skinned droid-spawn aren't welcome here."

"We come in peace. Your settlement isn't registered and we were simply investigating if you needed any assistance."

A young child shouted out from the throng. "You can assist by going the hell away."

A ripple of laughter rose into the warm air.

"We don't need anything from a bunch of aliens.

Now beat it, and tell the rest of your inky brethren not to come back."

"Humans are not native to this planet." I grimaced at Cazak's smarmy grin. "That kind of makes us ALL aliens here."

The sound of weapons powering up in the crowd had me thinking this could go bad fast. Ignoring Cazak, I bowed my head to the lead human.

"Then we go in peace."

I turned on my heel and walk back toward the ship, Cazak and Jalok falling in behind me. As soon as our backs were turned, a wave of open threats and insults was hurled at us.

A soft-bodied fruit smashed between my shoulder blades, setting juice running down my skinsuit, but I didn't even slow my stride.

"Sir?" Jalok looked at me with widened eyes, as if unbelieving that I didn't react to the hurled vegetation.

"As you are, Jalok." We got back inside the ship and the ramp raised up flush with the hull. I relayed the order to the pilot to take us up posthaste.

As our craft climbed back into the sky, my mind was troubled. I had a feeling that this settlement was going to be a thorn in the side of anyone who wanted peace between the species.

PHRYNE

I frowned and checked the time on my wrist device for the third time since the briefing was supposed to officially start. Twenty minutes had passed and there was no sign of General Rouhr's soldiers.

Personally, I didn't think we needed to wait for them. All meetings were carefully documented. The soldiers could catch themselves up whenever they deigned to make an appearance.

"Should we send a search unit?" Vidia reached over to General Rouhr, who sat beside her, and squeezed his forearm. Concern flooded her expression. I tried not to frown.

Vidia and General Rouhr made a great team. They worked well together politically, socially, and on every other level that mattered and quite a few that didn't. However, I'd never approved of allowing emotions to show through in a professional setting. There was a job to do. Becoming consumed with fear or worry wasn't going to help get that job done.

"Do you think something's gone wrong?" I asked.

"None of the team I sent out is answering their comms." General Rouhr's frown remained prominently on his face. "Vidia's right. Let's send a small search drone to their last location."

General Rouhr was about to send the order, when a brilliant pale blue light appeared in the room.

"Oh, hell no," I muttered.

Rift travel was a wonderful innovation that was slowly integrating itself into everyday operations. It was wildly convenient, if not uncomfortable to utilize.

However, it was meant to be impossible to walk through a rift into high-security areas like this one without going through the proper clearance procedures.

I knew the proper procedures hadn't been performed in this case because I was the person who approved the damn requests. I locked eyes with Vidia, who looked apologetic.

Yes, she technically was my boss but she knew how I was about this sort of thing. Control was key, especially in a tumultuous time such as this.

I reached for the weapon strapped to my side in case it was indeed a threat coming through a rift into our base of operations. I was ready to pull it loose and fire right up until a dark bald head appeared in the blue light.

A K'ver stepped through the rift portal. His expression was gravely serious. I took my hand off my weapon.

Naturally, it would've been a K'ver that circumvented the security protocols. I eyed the glowing lines of complex circuitry that lined his arms and the left side of his neck.

The light of the rift portal faded back into nothing and I was able to get a good look at the K'ver. His strong jaw was clenched. There was a somber expression in his solid obsidian eyes.

Something strange flickered in my chest.

My anger dimmed.

Something about this K'ver, though I couldn't put my finger on it, had caught my attention.

Maybe he reminded me of an old childhood friend from the orphanage. No, that wasn't it. Something else.

I shook the thought away. Now wasn't the time.

"Apologies for disregarding protocol," the K'ver said to me.

Clearly, he knew who I was, meaning we must've met at one point or another. Perhaps this was what

Vidia meant when she said I needed to work on my interpersonal relationships.

"I expect you to tell me why you did so." I lifted my chin and gave him a stern look. With the other aliens, the Valorni especially, it was important to physically demonstrate a lack of intimidation. Ordinarily, that wasn't a problem for me, but suddenly thinking of my time at the orphanage had thrown me off.

"Of course," he nodded. "General Rouhr," the K'ver turned away from me to address his general. "Our recon team was attacked at the old *Vengeance* landing site."

Even now, General Rouhr's face darkened with a shadow of sadness. Vidia gave his forearm another squeeze. I didn't understand the love the general had for his vessel, but then again, I'd never been assigned on a ship. Regardless, the loss of the *Vengeance* had deeply affected the general.

"What happened, Sk'lar?" General Rouhr inquired, the sadness gone as quickly as it had appeared.

"Anti-alien fanatics," the K'ver, Sk'lar, said with a dismissive shake of his head. "No injuries, but considerable threats."

"Do you think there's any substance to those threats?" I asked.

"Potentially," Sk'lar nodded. "This group was more

organized than others we've dealt with in the past. I wouldn't take anything they say too lightly."

"I expect a full report detailing the exact words exchanged," I said.

Sk'lar tapped a device strapped to his wrist that connected right into the circuits on his skin.

"Not a problem."

"Good." I nod curtly.

"I'd like that report sent to me, as well," General Rouhr asked.

"Obviously," Sk'lar nodded.

At that moment, a Valorni came through the door, out of breath and covered in a light sheen of sweat.

"I came as soon as I could," he panted. I'd met this one before, too, but his name escaped me.

"Karzin, what took you so long?" The hint of a smirk appeared on Sk'lar's mouth.

"I went through the proper channels," Karzin grumbled.

"Which is appreciated," I tossed in.

"Did you tell her about the anti-alien jackasses?" Karzin asked Sk'lar.

"You're picking up the local lingo nicely, Karzin," General Rouhr interjected. "Yes, we've been briefed on the situation."

"What are we going to do about it?" Karzin questioned.

"We should focus on preventive measures," Skit jumped in. "Completely suppressing them will only cause a stronger uprising."

I lifted a brow. Solid logic. Not bad, kid.

"Declaw them instead of exterminate them," Vidia said thoughtfully.

"They'll likely start acting out more as soon as election campaigns are underway," I said. "Vidia, you're the favorite among much of the population, but anti-alien groups aren't going to want you in a position of power."

Vidia, the former mayor of Fraga, ran Nyheim while our world rebuilt itself after the Xathi attack. During the crisis and its aftermath, Vidia slowly found herself at the helm of human government.

At the end of the Xathi war, the council invited her to carry on mayoral duties during the rebuilding period. She did so faithfully, rebuilding the city until it was ready for elections.

Now that things had quieted down, other prominent people from the pre-Xathi government wanted to go back to an electoral system.

Personally, I wished they'd leave it alone. Vidia had done a remarkable job keeping the planet on its feet after the Xathi invasion. She was clearly the best for the job, which is why I wasn't worried about her ability to prove it in an election.

However, I *was* worried about her safety, especially with all these anti-alien capsules popping up everywhere. I'd feel better if I had a headcount.

"I want you two in the streets," I said to Tona and Skit. "I want you in civilian clothes. Talk to anyone and everyone about the anti-alien bullshit. Keep a recording device and your GPS on at all times. I give you creative freedom, but we need an idea of how prominent these groups are within the city."

"Yes, ma'am," Skit nodded.

"Where are we with the food inventory?" General Rouhr asked.

Tona grabbed a datapad and pulled up a report.

"Our numbers are steadily improving," he informed us.

"That sounds like there's a 'but' at the end of that," Vidia smiled sadly.

"The Xathi destroyed so much. Valuable, fertile lands were destroyed and will take time to replenish. The land we can use is in good shape and the output is in the top percentile, but we won't be off rations by the end of the year like we'd hoped."

"Anything we can do to boost crop output?" the general asked.

"Not without using harmful agents."

"Can't do that," General Rouhr frowned. "The Puppet Master would be most displeased with us."

"Could we ask its permission?"

"If someone walked up to you and asked if they could pour acid on your arm, would you agree to it?" Vidia prompted.

"Point taken."

"What about the construction of new settlements?" General Rouhr moved on.

"The eco-construction is going very well," Tona reported. "That Puppet Master thing is an architectural genius."

"The fruits of the alliance are already showing," the general grinned.

"We could use that for the election," I spoke up. "Vidia played an active role in forming our liaison with the Puppet Master, and there's a clear link to a positive output."

"What matters is that the work gets done, not that I keep my power," Vidia said kindly.

"Having you in power is what's allowing the work to get done," I corrected. "It's in the best interest of everyone that you officially take the reins of the capital and keep our progress as a planet flourishing."

"If you weren't so damn brilliant with the security team, I'd have you writing my speeches," Vidia joked.

"I don't think I have the interpersonal skills for that." Vidia was one of the few people I openly joked with. I had a skill for keeping my professional life and work life separated, but I considered Vidia a friend.

"Fair enough," Vidia chuckled. "Besides, I'd rather have you there to keep me alive."

"Which is something we should discuss in further detail." I steered the conversation back to the issues at hand. "I'm confident Skit and Tona will find evidence of anti-alien factions growing bolder within the city, as well as within the settlements. I want to impose extra security measures here so we're prepared."

"What do you suggest?" Vidia asked.

"One of the trends I've noticed is that no matter how rowdy an anti-alien faction member is, they're hesitant to directly engage in combat. Correct?" I looked to Sk'lar for confirmation. He nodded.

"The anti-alien radicals understand that they are physically outmatched against General Rouhr's forces. We should allocate a defense team specifically for Vidia during the election period," I suggested.

"I think that's an excellent idea," General Rouhr agreed. "Sk'lar, what do you have your team working on lately?"

Sk'lar hesitated, which I found surprising. He didn't look like the type to hesitate.

"Routine patrols focusing on the old *Vengeance* site and the *Aurora*, sir," Sk'lar replied.

"I'm going to reassign your strike team. You'll be working with Phryne to ensure Vidia's safety at all times."

"Yes, sir."

SK'LAR

"I didn't blast my way through the crystal carcasses of Xathi excrement to be put on babysitting duty."

I glanced over at Tyehn as he fumed at my side. The overhead lights made his green skin shine as if wet. He was accompanying me part of the way to my meeting with the human commander Phryne Manka at the Nyheim central government building. His destination was the armory, where I hoped to acquire some smaller weaponry more apropos to guard duty.

"At ease, Tyehn." My tone belied the fact that I actually agreed with him. "Protecting an important woman like Vidia is a totally valid assignment."

His jaw worked silently, but he didn't offer further argument. The truth was, I felt much the same way.

Normally, guard duty was hardly the way to

establish yourself to the high command. But ever since we'd crashed on this planet, everything was different. Vidia was our commanding officer's mate, after all.

And no matter what, a command was a command.

We parted at the armory and I continued deeper into the winding hallways on my journey to Phryne Manka's office. When I arrived, I expected to find a receptionist, but instead found her door standing open.

At first she didn't notice me. Her wide eyes were fixed upon a multitude of datapads spread out on her otherwise pristine desk. There was something rather formidable about this woman, something I couldn't quite put my finger on. Though she only weighed half of what I did, my instincts told me she would be a canny and dangerous opponent.

I cleared my throat, a human gesture I had picked up. Manka glanced up from her datapads and waved me inside informally.

"Commander...Sk'lar, was it?"

"Commander Sk'lar it is." I offered a crisp salute.

"Well, Sk'lar-it-is, have a seat. I'll be with you in just a moment."

I sat down, frowning at her jibe, but she didn't notice. A moment stretched into minutes, and soon I grew bored with the wait. To amuse myself, I took in the sight of her red hair. We K'ver lacked such bodily adornments, and I was a bit fascinated with the way it swished about when she moved her head side to side to peer at her various documents.

Just when I was settling in for a good wait, she put down her datapad and fixed me with a stoic gaze. I returned it, look for look. When it was obvious that neither of us was going to give ground, she spoke.

"Your CO speaks highly of you, Commander."

"I'm pleased to hear that, ma'am."

"Oh for god's sake—just call me Phryne." She waved away my formality. "I can't stand getting all tripped up on protocol."

"As you will—Phryne."

"You did good work at that anti-alien settlement. Most men I know would have turned around and started busting heads if they got hit with this planet's equivalent of a tomato."

"I am not most men, Phryne." Why did I say that? It came out with much more bravado than I'd intended. Her scarlet eyebrows arched and she looked at me askance.

"Indeed. Your record speaks for itself. I can see why you've been given command of Team Three."

"I am happy to serve in any way I can."

She grunted and stared at her pads again. I leaned forward before I spoke.

"Ah, begging your pardon." I think that was how the humans phrased it. "But I was going over Vidia's itinerary, and it seems to me that there are some glaring omissions in security protocol."

"Glaring omissions?" Phryne fixed me with a hard gaze. So help me, despite my greater size, I felt like shrinking back, but I fought the urge. "I designed the security protocol myself, Commander."

I shifted in my seat uncomfortably.

"I don't mean to call your competence into question, Phryne."

"But that's what you just did." She sighed, and rubbed the bridge of her nose. "Look, Commander, I realize that you're good at your job, but this is my playpen. You'll just have to trust my judgment on these matters."

"I have been assigned to protect Vidia. I would be remiss if I didn't bring any potential threats to light."

"Fair enough. But let's just humor the human, all right? In fact, let's assume that I know what I'm talking about and have a lot more experience with this sort of detail than you, hmm?"

I struggled to keep my face placid in the face of her brusque arrogance. The K'ver were exploring the galaxy when the human race was still hardening the tips of wooden spears in a fire. But I held my tongue, because that was what a good soldier did. He followed orders, even if he didn't agree with them.

"As you wish, Phryne."

"Good." She flashed a mirthless smile and returned to her datapads. "Take your team and secure the next location Vidia is speaking at. You have the itinerary."

"Yes, Phryne."

She studied the pads for a time, then glanced up at me.

"You can consider yourself dismissed, Commander." She refocused on the work before her. "But do go ahead and send over a list of those 'glaring omissions'. I'm curious to see what you think you've found."

"Understood." I stood stiffly and offered a salute before turning on my heel and marching out of the office.

Securing the sight didn't take long. Vidia would be debating other candidates at an easily secured room in the government building. With weapons scanners, security monitors, and just plain old eyeballs, I believed we would be able to keep her—and her opponents—safe from any untoward advances of the anti-alienists.

Again, I considered it a waste of Team Three's capabilities to be put on simple guard duty, but I was determined to fulfill my obligations to the best of my ability. It would be the same if I were assigned to clean latrines. Pride had no place in the life of a soldier, even if—or especially if—they were in command.

I dismissed my team and headed off for some much-needed R and R. There was a cantina that catered to us military types not far from the government building. When I arrived, the sun had already set and the place was packed. In here, K'ver mingle with other species without incident. Some groups were even mixed, though for the most part, people remained voluntarily segregated.

That's when I spotted Phryne Manka herself. The human commander was sitting by herself at the bar, drinking a tall glass of carbonated amber fluid. I believed the humans called it 'beer'.

I'm surprised that they weren't put off by the fact that it closely resembled the look of their urine, but I should not judge.

I started to just ignore her, then realized it would be impolite not to say hello. Sidling up to the bar, I ordered a Pangalactic and waited until she noticed me. Her gaze snapped over, and a slight, crooked smile played at her thin lips.

"Sk'lar." She politely inclined her head.

"Phryne." I did the same. "How does this evening find you?"

"Honestly?" She scoffed. "I'm bored. Tell me, do you know how to play pool?"

"Is that the game with the slate cloth-covered table, the long sticks, and colored balls?"

"Yes."

"Never heard of it."

Phryne's eyes narrowed in anger, but a moment later she chuckled. "You're kidding, aren't you?"

"Perhaps a bit." My lips peeled back in a smile. "I am considered not without skill in the Terran game of pool."

"Great." She finished her drink and stood up. "Come on. I'm challenging you to a game."

"Very well." I downed my Pangalactic and followed in her wake as she headed for the row of pool tables at the eastern edge of the bar. "But I must warn you that my K'ver implants have increased my manual dexterity and hand-eye coordination to the point where a human will be hard pressed to defeat me."

She paused, looked me up and down, then continued on her way. "That almost sounded like you were talking shit, Sk'lar."

"I would never be so bold."

"Oh, I highly doubt that. Here, I'll rack, you break."

"No, as the challenged entity, I insist on racking. You break."

Phryne grinned and gestured to the table. "Rack away."

I set up the colored balls into their peculiar little pyramid. The truth was, I wasn't all that good at breaking. I could sink my shots, but sometimes when I broke, I slammed the cue ball too hard and ended up making a mess of the table.

Phryne selected a cue stick, then rolled it on the table, ensuring it was reasonably straight. Then she leaned over, thrust her backside out, and lined up a shot.

A sharp crack, and then the balls were dancing in a wild, zigzagging pattern across the table. She sank three striped balls and two solid, then glanced up at me smugly.

"I'll take solids. You need a handicap."

"A handicap?" I couldn't help but laugh. A waitress passed by and I took down two glasses of the Terran beer. "I think we both need a little handicapping."

Phryne was a master at this game. My enhanced reflexes allowed me to keep pace with her, but I soon realized it's not just about physical dexterity. The game was all about setting up shots, and Phryne not only knew how to sink her balls, she knew how to clog up the table so I couldn't get any easy shots.

She won the first two games, then I managed to emerge victorious—but only because she scratched on the eight-ball. The fourth game I won on my own merits, but at that point, she'd downed several glasses of beer and was most likely not at her full potential.

As the drinks flowed and the balls rolled, we both relaxed. I was discovering that, despite our obvious differences, a smile is a smile and a laugh is a laugh no matter what planet you're from.

Unless you're a Xathi. The thought of one of those bugs trying to laugh just seemed absurd.

Gradually we started standing closer and closer together. The bar was quite loud, and we had to put our mouths to each other's auditory canals in order to hear properly. When she spoke in my ear, Phryne leaned her head on my shoulder. Later she helped me line up a tricky bank shot and actually molded her body onto my own. The feel of her warm, soft skin was pleasant, more pleasant than I would have expected.

And her scent wrapped itself around my brain, haunting me long after she'd moved away.

Bit by bit, the other patrons left, until a none-too-pleased manager came to inform us that the bar was closed. We took in the sight of stools up on tables and a busboy busily mopping the floor, and heeded his word.

"That was most enjoyable."

She looked up at me and smiled, standing a little unsteadily. In fact, I was standing unsteadily, as well. The whole world seemed to be intent on twisting to the left no matter how straight I tried to stand.

"Yeah. You know what else is enjoyable?"

"Enlighten—" I let out a loud belch. "Enlighten me."

She laughed hard, eyes squeezing shut and tears pouring out of the corners.

"Oh my god. You are just too much."

"That is what she said."

Phryne stopped laughing and stared at me starkly with that intense gaze. Just when I thought I had angered her, she laughed anew.

"Nice. You've really picked up the human lingo."

"So what else is enjoyable besides drinking too much and playing pool?"

"Well..." she traced a line with her finger on my ample chest. "You'll have to come back to my apartment to find out."

With a sudden flash of heat, I found this guard duty assignment much more palatable.

PHRYNE

There was a dull ache throbbing between my eyes. I didn't want to open them. There was pressure on my chest like I'd fallen asleep with a thick table leg draped across my body. The pillow under my head wasn't the pillow I preferred to sleep on. My blankets were out of order. I had a very specific way I liked to sleep.

Memories from the night before flooded back to me in a rush. I'd drunk last night, of that I was certain.

I didn't drink often.

Correction, I didn't use to drink often.

Since the Xathi invasion, I'd found myself spending more nights at a bar. Of course, I was very careful about my consumption. Momentary stress relief wasn't worth any permanent, or even temporary, damage to my body.

Yes, I drank more than I should've last night. The K'ver was there, Sk'lar.

I beat him at pool.

Twice.

We had a fun night. I couldn't remember the last time I had a fun night like that. Vidia would say I've never had a fun night like that. But Vidia didn't know about the midnight parties at the orphanage. No one did.

God, was the last time I had a fun night really when I was living in an orphanage? What did that say about me? Nothing good, I imagined.

I squeezed my eyes shut as I threaded the memories of last night into something that resembled a coherent narrative.

I beat Sk'lar at pool. I drank too much. I walked home from the bar.

But I didn't walk alone.

Like a flashbang, the memory of my lips melded against Sk'lar's lit up my consciousness.

Shit, we kissed.

That wasn't like me. I didn't kiss people.

Well, I didn't kiss coworkers.

My job was a high-stress job. Of course, I occasionally sought out stress relief other than drinking.

I opened my eyes to look down at the source of the weight on my chest, though I already had a good idea of what I would find.

A dark arm shot through with angular blue lines of circuitry was draped across my torso. Sk'lar breathed deeply as he slept next to me. Unlike me, he was above the blankets. His shirt was gone.

In the low light of the apartment, only the faint glow of his embedded circuits illuminated him. He looked otherworldly as he lay there.

I closed my eyes and let out a sigh.

Of course he looked otherworldly. He *was* otherworldly.

This was exactly why I carefully monitored my drinking.

Aside from Sk'lar's lack of shirt, he still wore his pants and his boots.

I sat up a little to look at the leg thrown off the side of the bed and stifled a laugh.

He wore *one* boot.

When I reached forward to stretch, I noticed my arms were bare. I'd worn a long-sleeved top to the bar; the same one I'd worn to work that day. With a sense of dread, I peeked under the covers at myself.

I was covered only by my panties.

With a gasp, I clutched the bedsheet against my body.

I seriously needed to remember what had happened last night.

Ignoring the sleeping alien beside me, I closed my eyes and emptied my mind. I remembered walking back to my apartment with Sk'lar. Actually, I didn't remember seeing him, but I definitely remembered hearing his voice from somewhere behind me.

We were laughing. A lot.

Obviously, I'd invited him up to my apartment. That in itself was odd.

On the rare occasion that I decided to relieve some stress, I never did it in my own space. I always went to the other person's place. No one, not even Vidia, had been to this apartment. God, I really did have a lot to drink.

Or I was really enjoying my time with Sk'lar.

At some point, we kissed. I already knew that. But what else did we do?

Judging by his clothing, we didn't do anything more than kiss.

At least that was one humiliation I was spared. I liked remembering the sex I had.

With great care, I extracted myself from the bed. Sk'lar groaned once but didn't wake up. Good.

I made a beeline for my bathroom with my hands

over my breasts. I felt like a skittish teenager afraid of being caught. It was ridiculous.

I turned the hot water all the way up, fully prepared to take advantage of that luxury today. Thick white puffs of steam filled the room in seconds. I couldn't see the door anymore. In my steam sanctuary, I finally took a breath and gathered my thoughts.

Clearly, I had some kind of attraction to Sk'lar that only drunk-me was able to show. Talk about dysfunctional.

Why him, though? I barely knew him.

Yes, he was very handsome. Not just for an alien, for anyone.

What was so damn special about Sk'lar that he was able to break through so many of my carefully drawn lines in one night?

When the shower door opened, I nearly jumped out of my skin.

"Sorry," Sk'lar laughed. "I would've thought the head of Nyheim security would've heard the door open." Through the steam I saw him strip down, and I quickly looked away.

"I was thinking," I said in defense. "What are you doing in here?"

"I figured we could talk." He stepped into the shower even though I hadn't made room for him. For the first time, I hated the fact that my shower was so spacious.

"And you think now is the best time for that?"

"Of course." Sk'lar made himself comfortable under the stream of hot water. "There's no way to hide anything."

I summoned all of my will power in an effort not to glance down and failed. I looked away quickly but not before I got a sense of how well-endowed he was. Thank god for the steam. Otherwise, my blush would've been obvious.

"I meant that metaphorically," Sk'lar smirked. "Why the cold shoulder, Phryne? Not that such a thing is possible in a shower this hot. It's like the fires of Pystatheins in here."

"I don't know what that means." I turned my back on him to grab my soap. "And I'm not giving you the cold shoulder."

"You were the friendliest person on this planet last night," Sk'lar contradicted. "You were charming, funny, and a genuine pleasure to spend time with. I refuse to believe that person is only activated with alcohol."

"I keep a strict line between my professional and personal lives," I shrugged, uncomfortable with where this conversation was going.

Oddly, I wasn't uncomfortable at all with him being

in the shower with me. Some traitorous part my mind quite liked it.

Or maybe that wasn't exactly my mind…

"You aren't working right now, yet I'm talking to workplace-Phryne."

"What's your point?"

"I liked the person I spent time with last night. I'm eager to meet her again. But I can't meet her if you're going to put a wall between us all over again."

His words caught me off guard. Whatever response I was able to come up with died on my tongue. Something inside me shifted and the usual reserve I'd feel in a situation like this disappeared.

"What are you suggesting?" I asked.

"I'm asking you to not shut me out just yet." I felt Sk'lar's hands on my shoulders. My first instinct was to tense up, to pull away, but this time I fought through that initial instinct. One of the caretakers at the orphanage used to say that someone's first reaction was what they were conditioned to do. It was the second reaction that showed their truth.

My second reaction to Sk'lar's touch was to relax into his hands. I focused on how he felt, the texture of his skin and circuitry, the comfortable weight of him.

"Okay," I agreed. "I'll do my best not to shut you out. Yet," I added with a laugh.

"That's all I ask."

"But I can't compromise my professionalism," I said quickly.

"Anyone who's known you for longer than a moment is smart enough to not ask you to compromise your work. Besides, as of yesterday, your work is my work. We both need to do exceptionally well."

"For Vidia's sake," I agreed.

"For our sakes, too."

I looked over my shoulder with a frown.

"What do you mean?"

"Nothing." An easy smile spread across Sk'lar's face. "Now, I'd like to enjoy a little more non-work-Phryne before we go into the office."

Sk'lar and I quickly finished our joint shower and prepared for the day. All the while, we talked about non-work-related topics, which was a struggle for me at first. We kept it simple. We talked about the food we liked, places we liked to go, and other things normal people would consider, well, normal.

When we stepped out of my building, we'd each returned to our professional selves.

We were halfway to work when someone called my name.

"Phryne!"

I spun around, confused. I didn't recognize the voice. I didn't know many people outside of work.

As the woman moved closer, I recognized her.

Moira Constantine. She had lived in the orphanage, too, though she was eight years my senior. She aged out of the system while I was still a kid.

"Moira." A smile bloomed across my face. Seeing her was like seeing a distant relative. The orphanage was the only family I'd ever known.

Moira didn't smile at me. In fact, she wasn't looking at me at all. She was glaring at Sk'lar.

"I thought I heard somewhere that you'd made it to the top, Phryne. That you had a great life, a great home, and a lot of power. Figures you turned traitor to get it."

"What are you talking about?" I sputtered.

"Ma'am," Sk'lar stepped closed to Moira, who bared her teeth like some kind of feral creature.

"Don't you come near me, scum! If I had a blaster, you'd better be damned sure there'd be a cavity in your chest right now."

"I'm sorry you feel that way. Allow me to remind you that I have a blaster myself," Sk'lar said evenly. Moira paled and finally looked at me.

"Traitor." She hissed and spat at my feet before rushing away.

SK'LAR

Well-dressed members of all four species filed into the auditorium at an agonizingly dreary pace. Though frustrating for everyone involved, it was absolutely vital to security that we check each and every being for any sort of weapon.

The elections were still a month away, but the fervor had reached a high pitch amongst the electorate. Vidia and her opponent would soon stand at opposite podiums on the stage, each laying out their plan for the future of our shared world.

My team had been called in to beef up security for the debate. I had taken up a position near the front entrance, standing on a raised dais so I could easily survey the entire floor at once.

A commotion at the doors drew my attention. Rokul and Takar, twin Skotans, had been manually patting down guests upon entry, even though they had already passed through electronic scanners wielded by Cazak and Thribb, our chief engineer, and his assistant, Zarik.

Thribb had had a complicated relationship with General Rouhr. Like many of the crew of the *Vengeance*, he'd been desperate to go back through the rift that had been accidentally created when we came here, and return to defend our families from the Xathi.

That was kind of an understatement.

His zeal had pushed him to attempt to lead a mutiny.

It had failed.

General Rouhr had been within his rights to execute Thribb.

But instead, he had shown mercy. And while Thribb had been confined, he had begun the process of counseling and creating instances of contact between himself and the humans.

Thribb had made friends with several humans. He worked side by side with them. And he came to understand that, for the time being, we were residents here. Home was not an option for now.

Rokul's scales popped out, and a hiss escaped his

throat as he slammed a well-dressed Terran against the wall. The human's eyes widened in fear as Rokul said something I couldn't make out.

Putting my finger to my temple, I activated my short-range comm implant.

"Sylor."

"Here, Commander."

"Go take over pat down duty at the entrance. The twins are getting a little restless."

"Understood. What should I tell them?"

"Have them join Jalok's group near the podiums. They can stand there and look intimidating all they want, but they're getting too hands-on with their work at the door."

"Yes, Commander."

Sylor lumbered over to the entrance and spoke with Takar. Both he and his brother sent withering looks my way, but they did as they were told and moved to the back of the room near the debate stage. Sylor then began the pat downs. His sheer size alone should keep the peace, but if anyone got uppity, he was more than powerful enough to subdue them.

Iq'her and Tyehn were on a slow patrol through the room, roughly opposite each other as they circled about the milling throng. Iq'her's implants and Tyehn's comm would allow them to stay in contact even if they couldn't see each other. Hopefully, the two of them would be able to spot a problem before it fully developed.

They had their work cut out for them. Most of the humans who glanced my way were wearing a sternly fixed frown of disapproval. The overall mood of the room was quite tense, like the air right before a storm.

In order to allay any xenophobic outbursts from the humans in attendance, the moderator for the debate was a Terran. Dr. Evangeline Parr sat at a booth to the side of the podiums, going over datapads likely laden with different questions designed to spark intellectual but not inflammatory discussions between the candidates. Part of me rankled at the pandering to the anti-alienists, but at the same time I realized that every attempt must be made to keep the peace.

It took nearly two hours for every guest to be carefully screened for weapons before being shown to the assembly floor. There were a few seats for the infirm or VIPs, but most of those in attendance would watch the debates standing. That was not good for security; if there wound up being a rush toward the stage, someone could get trampled to death.

Of course, it was up to my team to prevent such a thing, if possible.

When Vidia Birch walked onto the stage, a chorus of

jeers rose up from the milling throng. Being the cool customer that she was, Vidia didn't react, but I could see the tightness around her eyes. She smiled and waved at the few supporters that could make their voices heard above the aggressive din.

Her opponent didn't get much of a reaction. He was a Terran male who I was unfamiliar with, but I had been assured by those more skilled in things political that he was a moderate who was not likely to garner much support from the anti-alien movement. He smiled respectfully at Vidia, and Dr. Parr banged a heavy marble globe onto a flat metal plate to signal for silence.

The crowd was rowdy and took several minutes to settle in. Parr wound up banging the marble several more times before the room was relatively quiet. I was a little bit worried. I hadn't allowed my team to bring anything but non-lethal weaponry into the debate hall. Crowd control could be an issue, but a worse situation, where someone got shot, could be avoided altogether. Doubt gnawed at me as I considered whether or not I had made the right decision.

Among those watching the debate from the VIP section was Phryne. I found my gaze lingering upon her russet head of hair. What would have happened the other night had I not passed out from inebriation? I had never been attracted to a member of a different species before. Of course, truth to tell, I had never been much attracted to anyone. Duty was my drug, and my lover, if you will.

Or it had been. Now I struggled with my own instincts to do my job instead of stare at Phryne like a wistful school boy.

Dr. Parr spoke into an amplification device on her desk. Her voice came out over the loudspeakers installed in the ceiling.

"Welcome all sapients. This debate will help us determine our leader for the next term. Ms. Vidia Birch and her challenger Mr. Roji Gowron will answer questions selected from submissions made by members of the electorate. Are the candidates prepared?"

"Yes." Vidia's voice throbbed with confidence, but I believed she was just as apprehensive about the tension in the air as I was. Quite a few boos greeted her answer, but Parr banged the marble gavel until there was silence once more.

"I am ready, as well." Gowron's smile was friendly enough, but there was a craftiness in his eyes I didn't like. Of course, to be fair, most politicians had that same cunning look, so I should probably refrain from judgment. Besides, my job wasn't to vote here, it was to protect both candidates.

"Very well, let us begin. Ms. Birch, you have the

privilege of answering first. One of our constituents asks what your plans are to deal with the food shortage, being as the Puppet Master won't allow for the use of fertilizer or other chemicals."

"That's a great question, Doctor." Vidia frowned as relentless boos echoed through the chamber.

"Shut up, traitor," shouted a man from the crowd.

Many others took up the call, and soon a steady *traitor* sing-song chant built up. My team exchanged nervous glances. I could see Takar and Rokul stepping forward, hands reaching for side arms I hadn't allowed them to bring in.

"Order." Dr. Parr slammed the gavel down again and again. "Order, or I will clear this chamber and you can listen to the debate via transmission."

That seemed to work, and gradually the chants died down. Vidia was unperturbed and went right into her answer as if a near riot hadn't interrupted her.

"As I said, an excellent question." Someone booed again but Sylor's meaty paw on his shoulder quieted him right away.

"It is vital that we in the government maintain a good relationship with the Puppet Master. We are literally walking about on his body right now, and it's only fair that he have a say as to what is done to it. I am pleased to announce that our efforts to improve food production and distribution have met with great success, and we foresee an end to this situation soon. Thank you."

More jeers started up, but they faded when Dr. Parr beat the gavel. She posed the same question to Gowron. The milquetoast man's smooth veneer might not have been incendiary from the outset, but he'd only finished about half of his answer when the crowd grew tumultuous once more.

"Gowron is a pussy." Laughter and agreement rolled over the rowdy humans in the crowd.

"He's a dirty alien lover."

The angry Terrans surged forward, pressing my security team back against the stage. Things were getting really ugly, really fast. I tried to find Phryne amongst the press of humanity, but I couldn't see her.

"Team Three, this is Sk'lar. Clear the room, now."

"But the debates have barely begun," protested Jalok over comms.

"Now. Before someone gets—"

One of the anti-alienists seized a chair right out from under a VIP and hurled it at the stage. The missile went wide of its intended target—Vidia—but it sparked the fervor into a full-blown flame. Suddenly everyone was shouting, pushing, shoving, and brawling amongst the audience. Rokul and Takar dragged Vidia and Gowron off the stage as more improvised weaponry peppered the stage.

"It's getting ugly, Commander." Sylor grabbed a brawling human by the nape of his neck, picked him up, and tossed him ten feet in the air to crash in a heap against the far wall.

"Use necessary force to subdue the crowd, non-lethal methods only."

"Leave it to you to spoil our fun."

"That's an order, Jalok. You are under no circumstances to rip out anyone's jugular this time."

A group of anti-alienists charged my position atop the lofty perch I had chosen. If I remained standing atop it, they might topple me. So I made a split-second decision and leapt off right into the middle of them.

Lashing out with feet, fists, and elbows, I spread broken bones and misery in a cloud about myself. Most of these agitators weren't trained soldiers, and it showed. One good punch in the mouth and they crumpled like tinfoil.

I wound up with a clear area about myself. I was just about to go check on Phryne when a medium-sized human stepped in front of me. Right away, I assessed that something was different about this man. His skin was glazed with a sheen of sweat, and his eyes flashed with a strange light I had never seen in a Terran's gaze.

Drawing up my leg, I snapped my foot forward in a vicious kick aimed at his solar plexus; a blow to a

Terran there would leave him crumpled on the floor, struggling to breathe, but very much alive.

My leg trembled from the solid contact, but the man didn't go down. There was no reaction at all, no pain and no fear. He charged forward and got a hand around one of my wrists, and the other around my throat.

I thought it would be easy to pry his grip away from mine; I outweighed him by eighty pounds, easily. However, I found that I couldn't budge him. His fingers continued to tighten around my neck, making it difficult to breathe.

My stimulator implant kicked in, sending a surge of amino acids through my bloodstream, which increased my fast twitch-muscle response. With difficulty, I pulled his hands away from my body, then snapped my head forward.

My forehead cracked into the bridge of his nose with a wet pop akin to dropping a wet towel on the floor. The man fell backward, splinters of bone thrust through the skin on his bloody face. When he hit the floor, the strange light seemed gone from his eyes, and he stared up at me in confusion.

Momentarily bereft of opponents, I checked the room and saw that Team Three had the situation nearly under control. Dozens of agitators lay prone on the floor, hands behind their heads as they were put under arrest. Civilian security bolstered our efforts, and soon there was nothing left of the riot.

Except, that is, for spilled blood, broken furniture, and a sick feeling in my stomach that the worst was yet to come.

PHRYNE

I didn't feel like myself as I walked into the conference room. General Rouhr was already there, his hand resting on the shoulder of Vidia, who looked like she'd shed more than a few tears over yesterday's events.

It wasn't like Vidia to cry. Despite her incredibly kind outward appearance, she was almost as stony as I was when it came down to it.

Tough as nails, she was.

That's a large part of why I enjoyed working with her. Vidia acted with conviction and was relentless, but what happened yesterday had clearly shaken her. It'd shaken me, too.

Sk'lar was there, as well. He said nothing to me directly but subtly nodded for me to take the empty seat next to him. I silently slid into the seat and gave Vidia a smile that I hoped looked encouraging.

The other leaders of General Rouhr's strike teams took their seats. A few human women entered the conference room, as well. I recognized Leena DeWitt. She ran the labs in this building. She, and her carefully chosen associates, pumped miracles out of that lab.

Beside her was a woman I didn't recognize. Though her hair was dark, she bore resemblance to Leena. A sister or cousin, probably.

Another woman entered and took a seat with the others. I recognized her immediately. Nesta Kane. At one point, I'd considered her a threat. She was a known criminal at one point, after all. Now she was one of our most valuable assets. Her links with the underground communities provided valuable insight to the daily struggle most people outside of our militaristic bubble had to contend with.

Sometimes I forgot that the average person on Ankau was far more worried about where their next meal would come from or if they'd get one of the dwindling jobs than any of the issues I faced day after day.

When enough side chatter drowned out the heavy silence of the room, I leaned closer to Sk'lar.

"What are your thoughts on all this?" I asked in a low voice.

"You're allowed to talk to me normally, you know?" Sk'lar replied. "We're teammates now. Communication is encouraged."

"Right." I bit my bottom lip. "So, thoughts?"

"We've seriously underestimated our opponents," Sk'lar said heavily.

"No one died. Those fanatics still haven't killed anyone." I said those words not just to make conversation, but to comfort myself. The security of the area fell to me and I'd allowed it to be compromised. I'd put Vidia in danger, I'd put Sk'lar in danger, and I'd put innocents in danger.

"What's that look on your face?" Sk'lar said.

"What?"

"It looks like doubt, but you're the most self-assured person I've ever met, so that can't be it." He teased me, complimented me, and inquired about my well-being all in one sentence. Impressive.

"I didn't do my job well enough," I said in a clipped tone.

"That's not true," Sk'lar countered. "You thought of everything. It's because of your instincts that we were able to keep the riot under control."

"I should've found a way to prevent a riot in the first place." I clenched and unclenched my fists at the sides of my chair.

"For all the measures you put in place, you couldn't

have controlled what a group of violent-minded individuals were going to do. Besides, I think there's an extra variable involved that we aren't fully aware of."

"What do you mean?"

That was impossible. I knew all of the variables. It was my job to know all of the variables.

"I'll talk about it more when the meeting starts."

"I'm your partner. Don't I get a preview?"

"We're partners now?" A smile flickered at the corner of Sk'lar's mouth.

"Direct colleagues," I corrected. "You know what I mean."

"I don't think I do. Enlighten me over a drink?"

"Really? Now is so not the time."

"I know. I'm just trying to distract you from digging your nails into your palms."

I looked down. My hands were balled into tight fists. I released them immediately. Angry little half-moons marred my palms.

"If there are no objections, I'd like to begin." General Rouhr stood up. He kept one hand on Vidia's shoulder as he spoke.

"First, I'd like to begin by offering my thanks to everyone who worked so quickly to apprehend the instigators of the riot. They are being held and questioned as we speak."

"Shouldn't one of us be down there doing the

questioning?" Vrehx, the Skotan leader of Strike Team One, asked.

"I specifically wanted everyone here for this," General Rouhr said. "The elections are still happening on schedule. We're not going to be intimidated by this sort of nonsense. But that means more gatherings like the one yesterday will be happening in our near future. The radicals will only get bolder from here on out."

"I have some observations on that front, sir." Sk'lar stood up. It was quick, but a look of surprise came over General Rouhr's face. Why would he be surprised? Wasn't it Sk'lar's job to have observations on this sort of thing?

I dropped my gaze in an attempt to stop myself from overanalyzing everyone.

"By all means," the general nodded.

"During the altercation, I fought one of the radicals," Sk'lar began. "I noticed the obvious changes first. The human male I fought was not larger than average, but well-muscled, and angry. It was obvious he'd received some kind of formal training more advanced than what we've seen in the past. Yet he was sloppy in combat. Not because of lack of skill, but because of his anger. It was bordering on unnatural. There was this odd look in his eyes, too. Does that mean anything definitive? I'm not sure. But his eyes were strange enough to draw my attention in the heat of combat."

"Did anyone else notice similar markers during combat?" General Rouhr asked.

"Everyone I fought was definitely bigger and stronger than any human I'd fought so far," Karzin agreed.

"Same for me," Vrehx agreed. "I didn't notice anything about the eyes, though."

"I think I have a theory." The voice of the human woman I didn't know was soft but still permeated the room. Everyone quieted to listen to what she had to say.

"Go ahead, Mariella," the general nodded.

"We first have to look at the situation from the radicals' point of view," Mariella began.

Everyone, including me, cast a doubtful look at her.

"Hear me out." She lifted her hands. "We have to remember that these people think they're the heroes of the story. If you were overtaken by an enemy much bigger, stronger, and more powerful than you, what would you do?"

"Get more power," Sk'lar volunteered.

"Exactly." Mariella turned to look at Leena. "What would an individual use to make themselves bigger and stronger? Something that also ups their rage threshold."

Leena considered for a moment before her face lit up. "Mari, are you thinking what I'm thinking?"

Mariella nodded.

"Care to clue us in?" The usual measure of humor was back in Vidia's tone. I couldn't tell if it was genuine or she was doing it for our benefit.

"Steroids."

"What's that?" Sk'lar asked.

I didn't know either.

"It's an old drug from Earth," Leena explained. "There were a few different kinds. It was used successfully to treat a number of human medical conditions when prescribed by a doctor."

"But there was a recreational element, as well," Mariella added.

"People would use it to make themselves gain muscle faster. It also had a tendency to make users irritable and more prone to fits of rage," Leena concluded.

"Sounds like what I saw," Sk'lar agreed. "But where would they get an old drug from a dead planet?"

"I can reach out to some of my contacts in the underground," Nesta offered. "Maybe someone there will know what the radicals are using to beef themselves up."

"If you find something, bring back a sample for me to test?" Leena asked.

Nesta nodded.

"Excellent," General Rouhr approved. "Now, as far as the election is concerned-"

"I've already told you, Rouhr," Vidia sighed. "I'm not giving up. These radicals aren't going to beat me and they aren't going to make me stop fighting."

"I can impose additional security measures," I spoke up.

"You're already doing more than enough," Vidia said.

"Clearly not if a riot was able to break out. We need to interrogate the instigators and up our security based on the info they give us. For the next debate, I want snipers posted at every viewpoint." I turned to Sk'lar.

"Load their guns with tranqs. If anyone starts something, take them down and drag them in for interrogation before anything can get out of hand."

"That's one possible plan, Phryne," Vidia said. "But what will that look like if I'm trying to present myself as an ally to the people but surround myself with armed non-humans? It sends the wrong message."

"Your safety is more important than how you're perceived."

"If I'm perceived as someone who will sell humans out to aliens, am I really any safer?"

I opened my mouth to speak but then closed it. "We'll form a plan that works for both of us once we interrogate the instigators," I decided.

Vidia nodded in agreement.

"That's all for today. Get some rest." General Rouhr

dismissed us before ushering Vidia away for a private conversation.

Sk'lar and I walked out together. When he turned to walk toward the exit, I followed him. Originally, I was going to go back to my station and read incident reports, but another idea struck me.

"Done for the day?" I asked him.

"Done until I get word about the interrogations."

"Want to go for a drink?" I asked before I could rethink it. Sk'lar lifted his brows in surprise.

"It's just that I could use a little fun," I explained in a rush. "I forget to pull myself out of my work and take a breath every now and then. It's bad for the job."

"Right." Sk'lar gave me a knowing smile.

"You're fun," I shrugged. "But I'd like to remember it this time around, if that's okay with you?"

Sk'lar chuckled. "Do you really think I have the power to stop you from doing anything once you've decided to do it?"

"Probably not," I grinned. "But it's been a surprising week."

SK'LAR

At least I wasn't on security detail. While running another supply drop wasn't exactly my idea of a fun assignment, it was better than security detail.

This way, I got to travel a bit, see what this planet had, and potentially meet new people.

Unfortunately, I was being sent to the Kangefi wetlands where the *Aurora* had originally landed months ago.

Fen and the other Urai, not being terribly fond of the heat of the desert, had moved the remains of the *Aurora* back to the wetlands using rifts. Apparently, the Urai preferred the humidity over the dryness.

Not that I could blame them. At least in the wetlands, they had trees and greenery. In the desert, where they had crashed during the final battle with the

Xathi, there had been nothing except tiny bushes and something the humans called 'weeds'.

They were green little plants that smelled disgusting, had tiny little barbs all over them, and seemed to grow everywhere after even a small amount of rainfall. Not to mention trees that could walk and tried to eat you if you weren't careful.

As Tyehn and I flew the supply shuttle out to the wetlands, I thought back to the riot. There was just something not right about what had happened there.

"Hey, Sk'lar?"

"What is it, Tyehn?"

"Why are we doing a supply run to the *Aurora*? Don't the Urai have their own food stores?"

I looked over at him. "They do, and since their digestive needs are different than virtually everyone's that I've ever heard of, they don't need to eat much. But they have a bunch of human scientists living with them, learning from them and using the Urai tech to study."

"Ah, that makes sense," Tyehn said with a nod. "I had forgotten that the scientists were still there, to be honest. I figured they had all left when Fen moved things out of the desert."

"Why would you think that?"

He shrugged. "They were studying the desert, last I heard. I figured they were staying in the desert after the Urai left."

I opened my mouth, then shut it.

It wasn't a bad hypothesis. The humans had been studying the desert, so with Fen moving the *Aurora* out of the desert, it made sense to believe that the humans might choose to stay to continue their studies. "I guess they figure that they can just rift over."

"I guess," he said as he turned away. "We're almost there."

I turned to look. What had once been a sleek vessel that looked more luxurious than anything I had ever seen before was now a small village.

Different sections of the *Aurora* had been turned into small buildings and were spread out. Little huts had been erected between each of the ship sections and a massive solar station was soaking up the rays of the sun to the western side of the village.

"Welcome to the village of *Aurora*," I said with a flourish of my hand.

"Really? They named it after the ship?"

I shrugged. "The Urai apparently aren't that imaginative with naming things," I answered.

"You sure it was the Urai, or did the humans pick the easy name?"

I pursed my lips. "You know, I'm not sure. Does it matter?"

"Not really," Tyehn said as he gently landed the shuttle in the small clearing meant for us. "Just curious."

I grunted. "Come on, let's get this stuff unloaded."

As we unloaded the boxes and crates of supplies, with some help from the 'natives', I noticed Fen walking over.

More like floating over. I would swear, all the way until my final breath, that even though their legs moved and it looked as though their feet touched the ground, they really did that simply to mimic the rest of us. The Urai were capable of floating across the ground, they had to be. No one was that smooth when they walked.

"Lady Fen. It's a pleasure for you to come greet us on a routine supply drop," I said with a minor bow. I didn't know why I always bowed to her, it just felt natural.

She returned my bow and spoke. I noticed that she no longer had to touch the voice box hanging from her neck to speak out loud to us. Actually, there wasn't a voice box hanging from her neck. It had been replaced by a small pendant half the size of my palm. "My friend Sk'lar. It is a pleasure for me, as well, to welcome you to our humble home. I wish to thank you for these supply drops. Our human friends will appreciate them."

"I'm grateful we can help," I responded.

"Maybe you could 'help' a little more," Tyehn grunted behind me. He was pulling a large crate from the shuttle and he was losing control of it. I rushed over and helped him balance it as we wheeled it out of the shuttle and onto the receiving pad. "What's in here?" he asked with a heavy grunt as we set it down.

"I think these are the replacement parts for some of their equipment that's been malfunctioning lately," I answered.

"That is correct, friend Sk'lar and friend Tyehn," Fen responded. "Tell me, is everyone in satisfactory condition after the disturbance during the debate two nights ago?"

"How did you hear about that?" I asked.

"I am in communication with Lady Vidia daily," came the answer. That seemed about right.

"Well, as for the humans, we still have two in the hospital dealing with injuries they sustained," I said in answer to her question. "Luckily, they aren't bad. Nothing a few days of rest won't fix."

"That is good," Fen said. "What about the perpetrators? What is the status regarding them?"

"Well," I started. "A few of them are still in custody. They're spending a little bit of time in prison, but they'll eventually be released. We don't have enough room to hold them all for too long, so we're hoping this keeps them out of trouble and calms them down a bit."

"I see." The Urai didn't have facial expressions, at least none that I'd ever been able to catch. And you couldn't really trust the synthetic voice that translated her thoughts to speech. But something felt off.

"Is anything worrying you?"

"Just concern for my friends' continued well-being," she replied politely. "But if there is nothing unusual in this encounter, than I shall trust all is as well as it can be."

I helped Tyehn move another crate before answering. "A few of them seemed stronger than humans usually are, but Leena and her sister seem to think the anti-alienists might be experimenting with old human drugs to increase their muscle mass." I frowned. "But that wouldn't explain the flash…"

"What flash?" Fen interrupted, her synthesized voice forceful and urgent.

"Uh," I hesitated a bit at this sudden show of emotion in her voice. "While we were fighting, there was a flash in his eyes, as if a flash from a bright bulb went off and reflected from inside."

"Are you sure of this?" Her voice was even more urgent now.

I nodded, then looked at Tyehn. His face reflected my own confusion.

What was happening here? Even some of the humans and Urai that had come to deal with the supplies looked at Fen oddly.

"You must examine that human immediately. Tell your doctors to examine the human's brain, and to examine as deeply as they can," she told me quickly. She then turned to the humans and Urai nearby. "Quickly, you must unload their supplies as quickly as possible." She turned back to me. "You must contact your medical personnel and examine those humans now. Have them send me a copy of their examination scans, as quickly as they can."

"Why?"

"Just make it happen. Go, use your shuttle's communication systems *now*, and tell doctor Evie that she must examine those humans' brains as deeply as possible." She was highly agitated now. She even put her hands on my shoulders and turned me.

"Go," she fairly shouted as she pushed me into the shuttle.

So much for not being able to show emotion.

I was confused as to what was happening, but I got to the shuttle comms and made the call. "Evie?"

"I'm here, Sk'lar. What's up?"

"I'm not sure," I answered. "I was talking with Fen about the riot and I happened to mention how my opponent's eyes flashed."

"Yeah?"

"Well, that sent Fen into a bit of a fit and she told me to tell you that you need to do an immediate brain scan of each of the rioters, as deep and detailed a scan as you can. Then send the results to her."

"Did she say why?" Evie's pointedly concerned voice came over the comm.

"No, she didn't. She turned me around and shoved me into the shuttle without answering."

"Wait, she touched you? She shoved you?" Evie asked. "Really?"

Tyehn jumped forward to answer. "Yeah, she did. I watched her push him. Hi, Evie."

"Hi, Tyehn," she answered. "Okay, tell her I'll start scans as soon as possible and send copies of the results to her."

"Thank you, Evie," I said. I clicked off the communications and looked at Tyehn.

He looked at me and immediately put his hands up. "Not me."

"Huh?"

"I'm not the one that's going to relay any messages to Fen," he said. "I don't want her to be agitated with me." His voice dropped. "She's always been a little spooky. This just bumped that little bit to a lot."

My shoulders drooped and I sighed. "Can someone just tell me what the skrell is going on?"

"You and me both. I'm going back to unloading. Nice, normal crates to unload." With that, he was out of his chair and back to helping with the unloading.

I looked out the back of the shuttle to see Fen

staring at me. Those blank eyes of hers were the most unnerving thing I had seen in a while.

I gave her a thumbs up, something I had picked up from the humans, and she nodded in return. She turned and walked away, leaving me more confused than ever.

PHRYNE

The moment I walked into work that day, I knew Vidia was up to something.

For one thing, she was sitting at my desk when I came into my office. For another, she was wearing casual clothes and walking shoes. I knew what she wanted the moment I laid eyes on her. I didn't wait for her to speak.

"Absolutely not, Vidia."

"I haven't said anything yet."

"You're going to ask me to escort you around the city," I supplied. "To which, I repeat, absolutely not."

"We used to do it all the time!" Vidia protested.

"That was before people started hating you for associating with aliens and doping themselves up on power drugs. Sk'lar returned from a supply run yesterday, with a strange report on the Urai. Everything is a bit weird now."

"That's hardly a reason to hide myself away," Vidia scoffed.

"That's the best reason to hide yourself away." I pressed my palm into my forehead. Vidia placed her elbows on the desk and smiled.

"Phryne, how long have you known me?" she asked.

"Since I turned eighteen." I knew where she was going with this.

"That's a long time." She leaned back in my desk chair. "I'd say you know me pretty well, right?"

"I suppose." I clenched my teeth.

"And when have you ever known me to shy away from something?"

"Never."

"Exactly." Vidia stood up and stretched her arms over her head.

"Are you about to tell me what an excellent opportunity this is?"

"Yes," she beamed. "The anti-alien radical bullshit will only get worse if someone else steps into power. I need to make sure people know that I'm not afraid of a bunch of bigoted morons hyped up on steroids."

"We don't know for a fact that it's steroids," I corrected. "It could be something far more volatile and dangerous."

"Could be. Might be." Vidia waved her hand in a dismissive gesture. "The point is, I'm not going to isolate myself from my passion projects and the people I'm trying to serve. Unless you physically restrain me, I'm going out to talk to people."

Vidia was testing me. We were about the same size, but years of military training gave me a distinct advantage. That didn't mean I wanted to hog-tie my only friend.

"Fine."

"Thank you!"

"But if I think anything is off the mark, we're leaving. No questions asked." I gave Vidia a stern look.

"No questions asked," she repeated.

"Does the general know about this?"

"He's just so busy with everything going on." Vidia wouldn't look me in the eye. "I don't want to add one more thing to his pile."

"You don't want him to freak out and say no."

"Exactly."

"You're terrible."

"I prefer to call myself determined."

Vidia and I left the office together after I changed into civilian clothes and loaded myself up with concealed weapons. I didn't tell her about that second part.

Many people recognized Vidia as we walked. No

one recognized me, but I didn't expect them to. I was much more of a behind-the-scenes worker.

Vidia stopped and spoke with anyone who wanted to converse with her. I smiled, nodded, and laughed when appropriate, so I looked like a friend, not a bodyguard.

We made our way toward the outer edges of Nyheim where the city had sustained the most damage.

The new buildings going up were stunning. The Puppet Master had advised the construction teams on the best materials. All the new buildings were made with a new type of eco-friendly carbon fiber. Tons of planters already filled with healthy green sprouts lined every available surface.

With a start, I returned my attention back to Vidia. I shouldn't have allowed myself to become distracted.

"Who will live in these homes?" someone asked her.

"The original owners of the destroyed homes will have the first pick," Vidia explained. "However, there will be more units than there originally were. Once the original occupants are taken care of, essentially city employees will be housed here."

"Like you and your friends?"

"For the people who work day in and day out fixing roads, keeping the power connected, and directing projects that will make our city thrive once more," Vidia answered smoothly.

"What about everyone else who's lost their homes?"

"There are two more developments just like this one rising up within city limits," Vidia explained. "We're using this neighborhood here as a test run, if you will. Ideally, the balcony gardens will grow enough food to sustain each unit and the solar panels will provide an adequate amount of power. Within two years, I want every building on Ankau on its way to being as self-sufficient as these are."

Her answer satisfied the people around her. As they fell into pleasant conversation, I scanned the surrounding area. Many people approached Vidia, eager to ask questions and talk, but there were many more who didn't. People hung on the periphery, watching but never approaching.

Some people looked mildly interested. Others looked like they were burning up inside. I locked eyes with a man glaring daggers at the back of Vidia's head.

He looked away but went right back to staring as soon as I turned my attention somewhere else. It didn't escape my notice that his arm muscles were so swollen they almost tore his short sleeves.

I tactfully moved Vidia away from the area.

The man followed. He wasn't trying to hide himself. With each step he took, his eyes never left the back of Vidia's head. He wasn't even aware that I was watching his every move.

"Sk'lar," I murmured into my radio.

"Ma'am." I fought a smile. Sk'lar had been respectful of my wishes to keep things strictly professional while on the clock. That didn't mean it wasn't funny to hear the K'ver who cursed the day I was born when I beat him at pool call me 'ma'am'.

"Please deploy my alpha team to the location of my comm. I'll stay in the area until I get confirmation that they've arrived."

"Yes, ma'am. Is there a problem?"

"Not yet. Can you scramble an aerial unit, as well? Put either Tona or Skit in with your pilot. They're both foaming at the mouth to prove that they aren't a thorn in my side."

"Yes, ma'am. Keep me updated, please."

"Will do."

I clicked off the radio channel and double checked that the GPS was working properly.

"Is everything okay?" Vidia asked.

"Noticing some suspicious characters," I replied. "I've called in a few extra eyes and ears just to be on the safe side. Don't worry, they know to keep it low profile."

"You say that now." Vidia rolled her eyes.

In the end, my point was proven. Once my alpha team was in place, I asked Vidia to point them out. She couldn't.

We walked around chatting and checking on the city's progress until the sun sank below the skyline. I insisted on escorting Vidia back to the apartment she shared with General Rouhr. He was waiting for us in the doorway with a stern expression.

"You couldn't have kept me more in the loop?" he fussed at Vidia as he ushered her inside. He looked over his shoulder and mouthed 'thank you' to me before shutting the door. For a big, scary alien general, he was completely mushy over his mate.

My heart gave a little skip before I returned to business.

"Alpha team, you can stand down," I said into my radio. My team members signed off, probably happy that their time was their own again.

I wasn't far from my apartment. When I passed the bar where Sk'lar and I were now regulars, I debated going in for a drink but ultimately walked on. Maybe I'd give Sk'lar a call. I wanted to go over details from the interrogations.

Suddenly, a sharp pain exploded from the back of my head. I stumbled forward, desperate to catch myself on anything. My hands wrapped themselves around a light pole, but that didn't do much to steady me.

Stars danced in my vision. I couldn't orient myself. I had no idea where my attacker was or where they'd strike me next. When the second blow came to my ribs, I lost my grip on the pole and staggered.

Damn it.

I took in a shuddering breath and gritted my teeth through the pain. I'd been trained to deal with this.

In front of me was a dark figure. Their face was obscured by a heavy hood. They wore a bulky coat, distorting their frame. When they moved to kick me, I countered. Ordinarily, I would've been able to knock them off their feet. Instead, I just made them stumble a bit. I didn't stop them from coming at me again. This time, I saw the glint of the blade in their hand.

The blow to my head had dulled my response time. I couldn't dodge completely. Instead, I rotated my body, forcing their knife to miss any vital organs or arteries. I saved my own life, but that didn't stop it from hurting like hell. I dropped like a heavy sack and lay very still.

Like I hoped, my attacker assumed I was too injured to do anything else. They ran away. Unfortunately, I still couldn't make out any identifying details.

Once they were far away from me, I carefully grabbed my radio.

"Alpha team, I need an extraction. I've been attacked."

I gave my location and carefully moved myself into a position that would do the least damage to my injury.

My attacker had sunk the knife between my rib and my arm.

One side of the blade nicked the skin over my ribs, but the other side sank deep into the underside of my arm.

Based on the sharp pain when I inhaled, they might've cracked one of my ribs.

No way was that attack random. Hundreds, even thousands of people had seen me walking around with Vidia.

As I waited for help, several theories popped into my head.

As if I didn't have enough to worry about already.

SK'LAR

I had just landed the shuttle from a second consecutive supply run to *Aurora*. Fen had given me a small data disk of her notes from the brain scans, as well as a new configuration program to help make the brain scans better, at least that's what she said it would do.

Security had been tightened in the last several weeks - with General Rouhr ordering that all governmental and military information that was classified and transported by either the *Vengeance* crew or the Urai be delivered to their respective counterparts in person.

I was to take it to the hospital and deliver it to Evie as soon as I landed. Being a delivery boy wasn't something that I had ever thought my life would be, but over the last two days, that's what I felt as though I had turned into.

At least it was better than spending every day wondering if today was the day the Xathi would finally kill me.

I took a small car to the hospital and went inside. I had to wait a little before getting to see Evie, she was in with a patient. Just under forty minutes later, she came out of the examination room, wished her patient a good day, and motioned for me to follow her. She led me to a small laboratory where there were a few doctors, Mariella, and Tella, all waiting for us.

"Hope this doesn't intimidate you," Tella said when she saw my raised eyebrows.

"Ease up, Tella," Evie said. "Fen called us, said you had something for us."

I nodded and fished the data disk out of my pocket. "This has her notes so far, as well as a new configuration program for the brain scan device," I explained. "She also told me to tell you that she wants copies of the new scans."

"As always," Mariella said politely. "Did she happen to tell you anything about what she saw or anything?"

I shook my head. "No. I think she realized that I wasn't smart enough to get all of the medical jargon, so she left it all in her notes."

"Okay," Evie said. "Have you been to see Phryne yet?"

I looked at her curiously. "What do you mean?"

"Aren't you and Phryne close?" Tella asked, putting a little more emphasis on the last word than the rest of the sentence.

"I guess," I answered.

For a second, Tella looked at me like there was something wrong with me. Then her gaze softened as she told me, "She was attacked last night. Someone beat the shit out of her. She's upstairs in recovery."

"What!?" I snapped.

No one had told me. No one had contacted me. I had even flown a mission out to Fen and her people and back this morning, and no one had thought to tell me this?

The last contact I had had with Phryne had been when she was escorting Vidia through the city and needed a flyover to ensure security. That was just a quick comm, nothing more.

Evie nodded as she came over to me. "She's in room twenty-eight. Go see her."

I nodded a thank you to them and left the lab. Instead of waiting for the elevator, I took the stairs two at a time and reached the second floor in a hurry. I went to the nurses desk, found out that room twenty-eight was towards the end of the hall to my left, and made my way there, trying my hardest not to break into a run.

I walked in to hear Phryne's voice at a level of annoyance that I thought was reserved strictly for stupid people. "Will you get the hell away from me? I'm getting dressed and getting out of here."

"But you need your rest and another test to make sure that everything's okay," I heard a high-pitched voice argue back. I pushed the curtain to the side to see Phryne getting dressed, pulling her shirt down while a nurse was glaring at her.

I saw the bruising on Phryne's side before the shirt made it all the way down.

White hot fury swept through me. Someone would pay for this.

But for now, my rage wasn't going to help Phryne, so I put it aside.

"Screw tests. Screw doctors telling me what to do. And while I know you're just 'doing your job'," she said as she raised her hands in the air and did the air quote motion, "screw you, too. I'm getting out of here. I have work to do and I'm fine. A few bruises are not going to slow me down."

"I can't let you leave without clearing it with the doctor first," the nurse insisted, her high-pitched voice sounding far too much like a child's to help provide any authority.

"Listen, lady," Phryne said in a huff. "I'm leaving. You can't stop me. The doctors can't stop me. Look, as long as I'm not dying from some sort of infectious disease, I'm getting out of here, okay?"

The nurse looked away from her in exasperation and spotted me. "How can I help you, sir?" she asked, grateful that she had someone else to speak to besides Phryne. Phryne turned around, saw me, flashed me a smile, and sat on the bed to put on her boots.

"I was actually here to see her," I answered, pointing to Phryne. "Is she giving you problems?"

"Like you wouldn't believe," the nurse answered. She quickly flushed as she realized that she'd said it out loud, looked back at Phryne, then shrugged. "She needs another day, she took a pretty bad pounding last night. We need to make sure that she's okay."

"I'll try to talk to her," I said quietly as I gently led the nurse out. "She's not the 'needing help' type, but I'll see what I can do."

"Uh-huh. Fine. If she ends up hurting herself more, I'll take some satisfaction out of knowing I was right," she nurse said as she left the room. With a shake of my head, I closed the door and walked back into the room.

"You okay?" I asked.

"Oh, don't you start, too," Phryne snapped.

I put up my hands. "Hey, I didn't even know you

were in here. Forgive me for checking on the well-being of a friend."

She looked at me, then smiled a sort of apologetic smile. "You're right. My apologies. You didn't deserve for me to snap at you."

"Accepted. Now, what happened?" I sat down on the bed next to her. The plan was to get her talking and hopefully talking long enough for a doctor to come in and order her to stay.

"There's not much to tell," she answered. "I was walking home last night when someone jumped me. Did a pretty good number beating the hell out of me," she added on at the end with a slight smile.

"Did you get a look at them? I can chase them down and..." I started to say.

She interrupted me as she shook her head. "I didn't see anyone," she said angrily. "They got the jump on me and knocked me down. I'm not even sure if it was just one person or two. All I know is I got my ass beat, I'm pissed off, I'm tired of doctors and nurses prodding, poking, and messing with me, and I want to get out of here and back to my job. I'll figure out who the bastard is that did this to me and deal with them."

"Oh? How are you so sure about that?" I asked.

"Not sure, but I'm pretty good at what I do. I'll figure it out," she answered.

"Any ideas who might have done this?" I was

starting to get angry, but since I couldn't pin it on an individual person or persons, there was not much I could do.

That just ticked me off more.

"No," she said with a shake of her head. "Probably one of those anti-alien freaks that's pissed off at Vidia and the rest of us for being 'alien lovers' or some stupid thing."

"Why didn't you let me know?" I asked her, letting my frustration drip into my words.

"Excuse me," she shot back. "I didn't think it was all that important to let you know that I got my ass kicked. What would you have done if I did tell you?"

"I would have come here, checked on you, then searched for the bastard," I said.

"Yeah, and you wouldn't have found anything, so you probably would have taken your frustrations out on the first idiot to say something stupid to you," she countered. "That's why I didn't tell you. Now, back off."

"Back off?"

"Yes," she nodded. "Back off. Leave it alone." She stood up from the bed and took a step away. I stood up as well. "Look, thank you for coming to see me and making sure I was okay. I appreciate that."

"You're welcome."

"Thanks. Now, I have a job to do and I would appreciate being allowed to do that job, okay? I'll do what I need to do, you go do what you're supposed to do," she said gently as she put her hand on my arm.

"But," I started.

She interrupted me with a kiss. It wasn't a kiss that had any passion to it. I was pretty sure she did it just to shut me up. "Stop. I didn't see them, so how are you going to find them, huh? Let it go. Okay?" Then she smiled and slapped me on the butt. "Look, if you're really interested in helping me blow off some steam, you can help me get my frustrations out tonight. If not, then that's fine, too. Bye."

She left the room, leaving me to sit there. Did she just? I was confused, frustrated, and angry. I wasn't sure how to deal with everything.

Despite the fact that I'd gotten lightly stabbed, the last two weeks had been great.

In fact, it'd been the best two weeks since the Xathi crashed through our sky and changed all of our lives.

Speeches, debates, and public appearances carried on as scheduled. Sk'lar and I collaborated to ensure a secure environment for Vidia to address the citizens of Nyheim.

In the end, my plan to use snipers armed with tranquilizers didn't come to fruition, but Vidia had agreed to extra security staffing.

We made sure to keep a healthy mix of humans and aliens to drive home Vidia's equality platform.

The real bright spot in all of this was that no riots broke out. I watched the crowds closely. Some people looked angry or disgruntled, but no one was brimming with insatiable rage.

Sk'lar and I normally went out for a drink after work twice a week. Now, as we sat side by side at the bar, was our fourth night in a row.

It'd become a ritual. It started out as a way to celebrate a successful public event. Now, it had become part of the daily routine.

And I liked it. Maybe a little too much.

"No matter what I say, stop me after the second drink," I told him.

"You said that yesterday. When I tried to follow your instructions, you listed all the ways you could incapacitate me," Sk'lar pointed out.

"I didn't list all of the ways," I rolled my eyes, "just most of them."

Sk'lar laughed and shook his head. I found myself laughing, too.

I liked this. Whatever it was.

I certainly considered Sk'lar a friend at this point, but this wasn't the same kind of friendship I had with Vidia. I wouldn't reach out and touch Vidia's arm when she made a joke, but I felt more than fine making physical contact with Sk'lar. In fact, I enjoyed all of our physical contact.

I liked the way his hands felt when they brushed

against mine and the way he always stood close enough for me to smell him.

"It's in your best interest to let me have more than two drinks," I went on.

"Do you think I'm trying to take advantage of you?" His grin was salacious and way too sexy for his own good.

I didn't put much stock into relationships. A committed partner was a liability in my line of work. If anyone wanted to hurt me, they could easily do it by killing my partner. As if that weren't enough of a reason, it was hard to find someone who understood all of the quirks that come with a person who was raised in an orphanage. I didn't think I had any quirks, but Vidia's told me that I do on numerous occasions.

That's one of the things that made Sk'lar great. He wasn't human. He couldn't judge me for my weird upbringing because he didn't have anything to compare it to. I bet his upbringing was just as weird as mine, if not weirder.

"You're doing that thing where you're too deep into your head." Sk'lar's voice disrupted my thoughts.

"What?"

"You're supposed to be working on living in the moment," he reminded me. "Were you thinking about work?"

"No, actually."

"I don't believe you."

"That sounds like a personal problem." I took another long sip of my drink.

"Cut her off after the next one, Clynt," Sk'lar said to the bartender. "There. Now it's his responsibility."

"Don't make me incapacitate Clynt."

"Tell me what you were thinking about."

"Nothing," I deflected. "Just how it's nice to have another friend. You might not know this, but I don't hang out with people that often."

"Really? I would've never guessed."

"Glad you've got the hang of sarcasm."

"Glad you're getting used to friendship."

I let the conversation fall into companionable silence. I could've said something about how it's nice to have a level of intimacy without any strings to get caught up in. Sk'lar and I hadn't done anything yet. Not really. But there was an air of intimacy around us that I was happy to bask in.

Uncomplicated and beneficial. That's how I liked things.

"They're covering today's debate." Sk'lar jerked his chin toward a glass panel mounted on the wall behind the bar. The footage of today's debate glowed in the dark space.

"Do you pay attention to all those speeches and debates?" I asked.

"I don't have the time," Sk'lar shrugged. "We're on high alert during those events. I don't get to listen much."

"Neither do I."

"Really? I'd think that, as Vidia's right hand, you'd know all of her speeches from memory."

"I'd like to," I admitted. "I'm not technically her right hand. I just manage security."

"You're her right hand."

"Fine."

"It's not bad to get close to people, you know?" Sk'lar prodded. "It's okay to acknowledge that you're important to Vidia."

"If I say something, will you promise not to get offended?"

"Even if I do, there are many ways you can make it up to me," he winked. My cheeks flushed. Maybe tonight I'd drag him back to my place and make sure he took off more than one boot.

"I've only been around aliens for a few months, but I always got the sense that the K'ver were very reserved," I said.

"You're not wrong," Sk'lar replied. "Skotans and K'ver are more reserved compared to humans. It's not part of our culture to be overly expressive."

"Yet you're quite insightful," I pointed out.

"Just because we don't openly express all of the

emotions in our repertoire doesn't mean we don't feel them and learn from them."

"Of course." I shut my eyes as I realized how stupid I sounded.

"My strike team and I are family," Sk'lar continued. "That's why we're able to be as effective as we are."

"That sounds a lot like the orphanage," I blurted.

"The what?"

Shit. I hadn't meant to bring that up. I didn't like people knowing I'd grown up an orphan. It invited pity. I had no use for pity.

"Orphanage. It's a place where children are sent to grow up after their parents die."

"Oh." Sk'lar frowned. "I'm sorry for your loss."

"Don't mention it." I curled over my half-empty drink. "I barely remember them."

"But there were others? And they became your family?" Sk'lar prompted.

"Yes."

"Then you understand what it's like for me and my team." He gave me a reassuring smile. I found myself smiling back. I could've kissed him for not dwelling on the whole dead-parents-thing.

"Well, how 'bout that," Clynt the bartender spoke, drawing our attention to the broadcast.

"What is it?" Sk'lar asked.

"A candidate just changed his whole platform."

"What?" I demanded. "Who?"

A man appeared on the panel. He was a portly individual with snow-white hair everywhere but the very top of his head.

"That's Dashiell Fox." I frowned. "He and Vidia never worked together directly, but they've interacted in the past."

"Friend or foe?" Sk'lar asked.

"I always put him in the friend category. What platforms is he changing?"

"Let's find out." Clynt walked over to the panel and turned off the mute. Other patrons complained about the sudden lack of music, but Clynt waved them off.

"It's come to my attention," came Dashiell Fox's voice through the speakers, "that other candidates would have us hand over our freedoms to the invaders. I'm here to tell you that I will not stand for it. That's why I've decided to change my campaign for Head Councilman. Our planet is a ship that's been caught in a terrible storm and it needs someone at the helm who will steer it back to calm waters. That starts with getting the invaders out!"

"Invaders?" I sputtered. "He can't be talking about you and the others."

"Sounds like he is." Sk'lar worked his jaw as he watched the panel.

"Vidia met with Dashiell last month. He wasn't anti-alien at all," I objected. "He shared many of Vidia's viewpoints."

"Apparently something's changed," Clynt commented.

Through the speakers, we could hear the mixed reactions of the people gathered around Dashiell Fox. They also seemed confused by Fox's sudden change in opinion.

"That makes no sense," I muttered.

"You're telling me," Sk'lar replied.

"It's not just the fact that he's switched to being anti-alien all of a sudden," I pressed. "If he wanted to do this, why didn't he step forward immediately after the riot and cash in on the tension? That would've been the smart thing to do. Why wait until after the threat is past?"

"Perhaps this is his way of stirring up trouble," Sk'lar suggested.

"He's only put himself at a disadvantage. Most of the planet is fine with having you, General Rouhr, and everyone else here."

Dashiell Fox finished his speech with a flourishing sentiment about human integrity. The applause that followed fell far short of thunderous.

The camera zoomed in on Dashiell Fox's face.

"Does he look all right to you?" I asked Sk'lar.

Beads of sweat were collected on Fox's upper lip and

forehead. His face looked unnaturally red, like he was under strain.

"Did you see that?" Sk'lar said suddenly.

"See what?"

"His eyes. Clynt, can you go back?"

Clynt messed with the panel and rewound a few seconds.

"Watch," Sk'lar instructed.

I started into the muddy eyes of Dashiell Fox, looking for anything out of the ordinary. Then I saw it, a strange flash.

"What the hell was that?"

"I don't know. But it's the same thing I saw when I was fighting during the riot," Sk'lar said.

"We've got to show this to General Rouhr and Vidia. This could be something huge."

I knew the two weeks of peace were too good to be true.

SK'LAR

General Rouhr and I stood near his office window, staring down at the cluster of activists clogging the streets. Some of them were carrying signs scrawled with anti-alien propaganda. Security forces maintained a close watch on the group, but they had gotten cagier since the brawl during the debates. No one made an overt enough call to violence to get themselves detained.

"Unreal." Rouhr's voice rumbled from his barrel chest. The scar on his face made his scowl all the more imposing as the activists marched past. "Don't these fools realize that in order to survive here we all must pull together?"

"Emotion often overrules reason in humanity." I

winced, realizing that Rouhr himself was involved with a member of the Terran species. "Sorry, sir."

"Don't be. You said nothing inaccurate." A brief grin flashed over his face before the shouting below melted it away. "Although I believe that particular failing is not just limited to the Terrans."

"True enough."

Gradually, the march moved on out of our view, flanked by security forces. We continued to stand watch in silence for a time, lost in our own thoughts. The general broke the respite first.

"That's the third protest in two days."

I nodded grimly. "The anti-alien movement appears to be gaining steam. I'm afraid that Dashiell's sudden change of heart has emboldened them."

"We cannot lay all of this at the candidate's feet." Rouhr turned to regard me, an inscrutable expression on his craggy face. "It is always easier to sell hate and fear rather than reason and cooperation. The history of dozens of sapient worlds bears that out."

I grunted and turned to watch the sun as it sank toward the horizon, casting red gold light over the sleek buildings.

"I admit I found the idea of alliance with other species to be...distasteful. At first."

Rouhr laughed softly and arched an eyebrow at me.

"And now? Do you still harbor such resentments?"

"No. My time leading team three has taught me that members of all species can be helpful...or, to use a Terran phrase, an enormous pain in the ass."

Rouhr gave in to full-on mirth, and even clapped a hand on my shoulder.

"Ah. And here I thought it was your dalliance with the lovely Commander Manka that changed your perceptions."

I looked at him sharply, my heart rate increasing. What had people been saying? Had Phryne been speaking about me without my knowledge?

Rouhr chuckled and held up his hand, palm outward.

"Relax, Commander Sk'lar. No one is gossiping about you and Phryne. It's just obvious to those of us who have experienced such attraction."

This whole conversation made me uncomfortable, so I changed the subject.

"I am still bothered by Dashiell's sudden reversal of position."

Rouhr indulged me and dropped the previous discussion.

"As am I. Not only that...the venom, the vitriol which he spewed is vastly out of character for him. I've met the man, attended government get-togethers with him. He's never so much as batted an eye at other species sharing his space."

"Not only that, but his eyes had the same glow I saw during the riot at the debate. Do you think that there is some sort of environmental factor? Perhaps spores or something from the local flora and fauna?"

Rouhr pursed his lips, eyes narrowing as he considered my words.

"I certainly hope not. Our alliance with the Puppet Master should prevent things of that nature from occurring."

"Assuming he—it—is being on the up and up with us."

Rouhr sighed and rubbed his eyes, seeming quite tired all of a sudden.

"We have to proceed from the position that it is playing straight with us. Unless there is incontrovertible proof to the contrary, the Puppet Master is our ally."

That shut down any argument I might have made, but I couldn't just let the notion go.

"Is it a possibility that this phenomenon is occurring without the Puppet Master's direct involvement? Some sort of genetic abnormality that makes certain individuals vulnerable to the environmental factors?"

"Perhaps." Rouhr shook his head and seemed to sag, as if bearing a heavy weight. "But in my completely unverified opinion, I believe this is all too convenient to be written off as chance or coincidence."

"Yes. Every time, it's been a human who has been affected."

"I was thinking more along the lines that every outburst has only served to help the anti-alien movement."

I closed my mouth while I pondered his words. He was right, of course, but that didn't do anything to allay my concerns. It only raised new ones.

"I suppose we shall have to wait until Fen completes her research."

Rouhr turned away from the window and walked behind his desk, settling into his chair with palpable relief. I wondered if he'd been sleeping at all lately.

"Indeed. Until she does, I am afraid I simply cannot decide on a course of action. Without her information, we cannot take any further decisive steps."

I remained at the window, watching the sun creep down below the horizon, while Rouhr picked through various datapads on his desk. I was sure both of our thoughts were equally troubled.

Oddly, Phryne's red-maned face kept popping into my head. Was what we had purely physical?

I'd thought so at first, but now I was uncertain.

Surely she would not linger in my thoughts so much without some further connection? Or was I being a fool, imagining different parameters for our relationship than actually existed in reality?

I knew I wanted her. Wanted to be with her, wanted her to be safe and happy.

But what did all of that mean?

My musings were interrupted by a loud, dissonant chime from the comm unit on Rohr's desk. I recognized it as a priority alert. He quickly activated the receiver, concern knitting his scarred brow.

"This is Rouhr. Report."

"General, we're receiving a priority-one request for assistance from Einhiv. An anti-alien protest has grown violent and local security are struggling to maintain control."

I stepped away from the window, adrenaline already starting to flow.

"I can gather my team in minutes."

Rouhr nodded and spoke into the comm.

"Prepare to open a rift to Einhiv for Team Three—"

"No, belay that order."

Both of us jerked our heads toward the comm unit in confusion. Not because we didn't recognize the voice—Fen's particular diction was hard to forget—but because she'd just countermanded the order of the highest-ranking officer on the planet.

"Explain yourself, Fen." Rouhr, to his credit, didn't seem angry at the counter-command, just confused.

"I don't have time to go into it right now, but opening a rift would be extremely dangerous. Einhiv will just have to wait for reinforcements the old fashioned way."

I opened my mouth to argue, but Rouhr held up a hand to stop me.

"Very well, Fen. I trust your judgment in this matter."

"Thank you, General. I wouldn't do this if it weren't absolutely vital."

"Sir, with all respect, lives could be lost before we mobilize traditional transport to Einhiv."

"I am aware of that, Sk'lar, but I'm also aware of the fact that Fen never does anything without a good reason. Team One is on maneuvers in that vicinity. I will dispatch them to deal with this crisis."

He relayed the order while I paced about, eager for action. As soon as his call was done, I spoke once again.

"General, we must find a resolution to this phenomenon, and soon."

"Agreed."

"Should we speak with Fen, then?"

He shook his head slowly.

"No, if she didn't have time to speak over comms, I don't want to disturb her research further. But there is another expert in the field of human biologics we can confer with."

"You mean Dr. Parr, don't you?"

"The same." Rouhr rose from his seat and

straightened his uniform with a downward jerk of his hands. "Come, Commander. Let's see what Evie can tell us about this situation."

I fell into step beside him, hoping that Dr. Parr could provide enlightenment. I'd much rather be busting heads with my team in Einhiv, but orders were orders.

PHRYNE

"Evie's making me come in for a checkup," Vidia announced as she strolled into my office that afternoon.

"Why are you telling me?" I asked without looking up.

"Because if I need one, that means you need one. We got ours together last year, remember?"

"No, I don't. How do you remember that?"

"Because I'm diligent about the health of my friends."

"Friends or the person that keeps you from getting killed every other day?"

"You're both. Come on."

"I can't." I gestured to the stack of datapads on my desk. "I have all these reports to go through."

"You sound just like Rouhr." Vidia rolled her eyes. "Want to know something cool about datapads? You can pick them up and carry them out of the office. Let's go."

Evie Parr was waiting for us when we walked in.

"You owe me ten credits," Vidia said to Evie with a proud smirk.

"Damn it."

"What are you talking about?" I asked.

"Evie didn't think I could get you to walk away from your desk in under twenty minutes," Vidia explained.

"Only because I brought my desk with me." I held up three datapads to prove my point.

"Doesn't matter. I still win."

Now that the wager was solved, I hunkered down in a chair while I waited for Evie to examine me. However, she didn't get the chance.

General Rouhr and Sk'lar strode into the clinic.

"Hello, darling," Vidia beamed. General Rouhr leaned down to kiss the top of her head. I was used to them subtly touching one another in meetings or during speeches, but I'd never seen them display this level of affection so openly. I felt a pang of something in my chest that I couldn't identify. I wasn't disgusted with them, but I was uncomfortable. A little hollow.

I was jealous.

My gaze was drawn to Sk'lar. He watched me with a careful gaze.

"Is something wrong?" I asked.

"I wanted to see if Dr. Parr had any results from those scans Fen had requested." General Rouhr explained. "But if she's busy, I wouldn't mind speaking with you more about the Dashiell Fox developments."

"He and his followers are strange," Sk'lar added.

"In what way?"

"We're noticing a lack of activities you'd call normal," General Rouhr said.

"Tell me everything," Vidia insisted.

She and Rouhr bent their heads together over the datapad in his hand.

"You and the general both had to come in here for that?" I questioned Sk'lar.

"Not quite." Sk'lar pulled up a chair and sat down next to me. "Something strange happened just now."

"What?"

"I asked Fen to open a rift and she wouldn't do it. She disabled the AI that allowed automatic rift creation based on our commands. She said it was too dangerous."

"Too dangerous? What happened?"

"I don't know. She disconnected."

"Does General Rouhr know?" I asked.

"He was there," Sk'lar shook his head. "We don't

know how this is connected, or if it is, but it's one more oddness to add to the pile."

"I don't like oddness," I mused. "Surely the general can make her tell him what's going on?"

"I'm not fond of the situation either," Sk'lar agreed. "However, the Urai tech is invaluable to us, and they like their independence. Fen's never let us down before, so General Rouhr's willing to give her the benefit of time."

"What are you going to do?"

"At the moment, there's nothing much I can do." Sk'lar rubbed the back of his neck. I noticed how the lights from his circuitry pulsed and flickered when he moved. "I'll admit, I'm getting restless."

"This is the part where you invite me to the bar," I grinned.

"I'm becoming predictable."

"Only a little. I'm still going to say yes, though."

We stood up to leave. Vidia called out to me.

"You haven't been examined yet!"

"I'll get my examination done tomorrow."

"I no longer owe you ten credits," Evie said to Vidia.

Sk'lar and I strode out of the building. I was shocked to see that night had fallen. Where had the day gone?

"Are you aware of how much time you spend in the office?" Sk'lar asked.

"I do my forty hours like everyone else," I shrugged.

"Try closer to eighty," he corrected.

"How would you know?"

"I pulled up your timesheet."

"Oh yeah? How many hours a week do you put in?"

"About the same," Sk'lar laughed. "That's why I need to come here so often."

We walked into the familiar dim lighting of the bar. Clynt stood making drinks like he always did. The same broadcasts were playing on the mounted panel. A group of three men was already playing pool.

"Looks like I won't be able to kick your ass tonight," I pouted.

"I let you win."

"Bullshit."

"You're too drunk to remember."

We sat at our usual stools and ordered our usual drinks.

"This might just be my favorite part of the day," I grinned.

"Is that because of me or because of the alcohol?"

"If I didn't know better, I'd think you were calling me an alcoholic."

"You spend the majority of your nights in a bar with me," Sk'lar pointed out.

"That's only been happening since I met you," I said.

"That must mean I'm something special," he smirked.

"Yeah." My voice came out softer than I wanted it to. I sipped my drink, but still wasn't able to hide my smile.

"There's something here. You know that, don't you?"

"Where?"

"Here." Sk'lar gestured to the half foot of space between us. "We both feel it."

"Maybe there is. So what?" I was baiting him. There most certainly was something there, something more than I'd been willing to admit.

"I think it's time we do something about it."

"Like what?"

"Follow me."

Sk'lar wordlessly got up from the bar. I followed him.

"I'll just put those on your tabs, then?" Clynt called after us.

"Put both drinks on mine," Sk'lar called over his shoulder.

We didn't speak as we walked back to my apartment or when we took the elevator up to my floor. It wasn't until we stood in the center of my living space, so close that my chest grazed against his when I took a breath, that he finally spoke again.

"Do you remember the last time we did this?"

"I reckon I remember more than you do. We kissed. It was glorious. And then you passed out and began to snore."

"You're right. We're not going to count the first time we did this anymore. This is our first time now."

His hands settled on my waist and pulled me in closer, so that my chest was flush against his.

I wanted to say something funny or witty. Something to make this moment lighthearted and meaningless like all of our other moments had been. But this moment meant something. I felt it.

When he brought his lips to mine, I took in every sensation. I was so focused on his mouth that I didn't notice he was moving me backward until my legs hit the bed.

I let myself fall back, pulling him down with me. With eager hands, I pulled his shirt over his head. He moved his hand under me and lifted my back off the mattress before removing my shirt. He didn't set me down right away. Instead, he held me against him. I wound my arms around his neck, locking my body against his. With light fingers, I traced patterns across his skin and played along the lines of his complex circuitry.

When he crushed his lips down on mine, there was a fire that hadn't been there before. I parted my lips and allowed the kiss to deepen. He moved so that his hips were wedged between my legs. I felt the evidence of his arousal pressing against my inner thigh.

Well endowed, just like I'd suspected that time in the shower.

"I'm very glad I didn't shut you out," I whispered in his ear before gently biting down on his earlobe.

"Me, too."

He took away the hand on my back, letting me fall back onto the mattress. His hands moved down my stomach to my hips. With one swift motion, he pulled down my pants and underclothes. He paused to take off my boots before removing every article of my clothing.

When he moved back up my body, he stopped at my thighs. I let my head loll back onto the bed while he kissed his way up my inner thigh.

I wasn't expecting to feel his mouth at the apex of my thighs. He paused as if asking for permission.

I nodded, breath catching in my throat.

Every gentle, probing stroke of his tongue tore a sigh from my lips. When his clever mouth moved up my stomach, I almost grabbed his head and pushed him back down.

Anticipation quivered through my body as I waited to see what would come next.

He stopped at my breasts. As he kissed them, I watched the glow from his circuits illuminate my skin.

I sat up just enough so that I could reach his belt. I undid the clasp and pushed his pants down. His swollen member pressed against my slick folds, sending electricity shooting through my body at just this touch.

"Ooh," I gasped as, with tantalizing slowness, Sk'lar entered me.

Our eyes locked on each other's while my body adjusted to his girth.

"How's that, Phryne?" he asked, lips brushing over mine.

Too filled with unexpected emotion to speak, I rocked my hips up into him and silently begged for more. With a hungry edge to his gaze, his hips bucked against me, each impact sending an explosion of pleasure through my body.

Without warning, he took both of my calves and lifted them one after the other so that my legs were slung over his shoulders. He sank deeper inside me. I cried out, not caring if anyone heard me.

I wrapped my arms around him and pushed my face into his neck as my body gave way to shakes and trembles. I tightened around him, excruciatingly aware of every inch of him inside me. My breaths came in short, hard bursts and my pleasure reached its peak and crashed back down over me.

The world spun on its axis as we climaxed together. I was aware of nothing, not the bed beneath me nor the ceiling above me.

Nothing except Sk'lar.

SK'LAR

The implant never had a chance to awaken me at dawn, because the delectable smell of food preparation wafting into my nostrils beat it to the punch. Sitting up in bed, I rubbed my eyes and yawned. Part of me wondered if I was getting far too comfortable with waking up at Phryne's apartment.

My lips stretched in a smile when I recalled the events of the previous night. Making love deep into the night with an enthusiastic partner might be the best way to spend an evening I'd yet encountered.

And with Phryne, sweet, tough, irresistible Phryne, I'd never get enough.

It only took me a moment to don my skintight undergarment, then I walked barefooted and bare chested into Phryne's kitchen. She stood before the stove, humming to herself, clad in a miniscule undergarment with mere strings holding it around her waist. The thin strip of fabric covered nothing, instead disappearing between her small but well-shaped rear cheeks. I remembered that last night, at some point, I'd tried to count the freckles adorning her bottom—with my tongue.

Other than the almost-panties, Phryne was clad only in a thin sleeveless shirt. For a while, I enjoyed just standing there and watching her move about the kitchen while so scantily clad. My body responded to the idea of taking her back to bed. But in this case, my empty belly overruled my sex organ—at least for now.

Phryne turned around, bearing a steaming skillet full of some crispy, greasy meat, and noticed me at last. A slight smile played about her lips and a rosy blush adorned her cheeks.

"Good morning."

"Good morning." My voice was still thick with recent slumber, but Phryne didn't seem to mind. In a few short steps, I was nestled against her, embracing her from behind. Phryne moved her skillet back to the stove, chuckling all the while.

"Hold up, you ape, you're going to make me dump our breakfast all over the floor."

"Then I'll have to eat something else."

For emphasis, I put my mouth on her shoulder and started working toward her neck. She wriggled that magnificent bottom across my crotch, springing me into greater arousal. Then the little tease broke out of my grip and returned to her culinary task at hand.

I let out a frustrated grunt, even though a smile remained fixed on my ebony face.

"Patience, big guy. There's plenty of time for that later."

"I'll hold you to that." She seated me at the dining table and placed a plate of steaming protein and vegetables in front of me. After getting herself a similarly laden platter, Phryne sat opposite me and dug a fork into the mound.

My first bite sent explosions of fiery flavor across my tongue. K'ver food tended to be practical, like us. Food was prepared with an eye to nutrition first, palatability a distant second. Humans, however, considered the preparation of cuisine to be an art form all in itself. Tasting Phryne's cooking, I couldn't help but agree.

"What do you think?"

Glancing across the table, I found Phryne staring at me expectantly. I felt that she was more worried about my answer than any of the craziness which had enveloped our world.

"It's delicious." I took another bite for emphasis. "It sort of burns my mouth, but I don't mind at all."

"That's the jalapeno peppers. I understand it was damn hard to get them to grow on this planet, but worth every drop of sweat."

"Indeed." My napkin was repurposed to wipe my glistening brow. "In more ways than one."

We returned to our food and, for a time, the only sounds were the clink of dinnerware against ceramic plates. At length, I looked up to find her watching me intently again.

"What's the matter?"

"Nothing. It's just—sometimes you seem really... otherworldly. Even when you're doing something familiar to me, like eating."

"Hmm." I took another bite and spoke around the mouthful. "I suppose that's because, from your perspective, I am otherworldly. Even though we are both of the K'veri endotype, there are—"

"Wait, did you say K'veri endotype?"

"Yes." I set my fork down. "I mean, you have two locomotive limbs, two manipulatory limbs, one head and—why are you laughing?"

Phryne dabbed at her mouth and shook her head, tears welling in her eyes.

"I'm sorry, it's just kind of odd. But it makes sense.

We would classify your species as 'humanoid', which means basically the same thing. I guess it's all a matter of perspective."

"Indeed." I smiled, not quite getting why this was funny but enjoying her mirth nonetheless. "I suppose it's quite fortunate that our species are so...compatible."

"Yes, it is." There was a gleam in her eyes that made my heart race. "We should—explore—this compatibility further, don't you think?"

I stood up, intent on crossing the kitchen and taking her lithe form in my arms, when I became aware of an insistent chime. Racing back into the bedroom, I found my external comm unit flashing with a priority alert.

"What's wrong?"

I turned to find Phryne standing in the doorway, leaning on one arm. The position had lifted her upper garment, revealing the underside of the pink mounds of her breasts. Regret coursed through me, but orders were orders.

"I have to report to the airfield immediately. Team Three is needed."

She smiled, only the slight tightening at the corner of her eyes betraying her worry as I raced about the room, gathering up my garments.

"Well, I suppose we'll have to take a rain check."

"A rain check? What is that?"

"It's—it just means we have to wait."

"I see." I didn't, but I didn't have time to make further inquiries on this 'rain check'.

Phryne and I shared a long, lingering kiss at the door, and then I rushed to the airfield. My legs were just starting to burn when I reached the tarmac.

I kept up the steady pace, passing by sleek craft until I spotted General Rouhr, dressed out in full battle gear. For a split second, I thought I was about to be relieved of command, then I dismissed the notion.

"Sk'lar." Rouhr gestured to the waiting *Ripper*-class armored transport. "Your team awaits its leader."

"What's the situation, General?"

"I received a cryptic distress call from the *Aurora*. Fen still refuses to allow anyone to rift, so this is the speediest way to get boots on the ground."

"Right. No idea what we're dealing with? More of the anti-alien activists?"

"Unknown."

We raced up the ramp, metal clanking with each footfall. Team Three was already strapped in, geared up and ready to lift off. Jalok whispered something in Cazak's ear, and the two of them enjoyed a good chuckle.

"Be serious in the presence of the general!" I bellowed. "He's coming on this mission with us!"

"At ease, Sk'lar," the general replied. "Team Three

may be what the humans term "cowboys", but camaraderie before battle is to be cherished, even in the presence of a general. Besides, I think this time the mirth is caused by you."

So. The gossip had reached everyone's ears, it seemed, and every single person on this craft knew where I'd spent the previous evening.

At least Tyehn was all business, but I knew that was more because he couldn't wait to fight rather than out of any sense of preserving my dignity.

"Any clue what we're going to face, Commander?"

"None. But we're going in hot this time."

"Music to my ears."

We all lurched in unison as the craft tore itself away from the ground. There were no windows in an armored transport like this, other than in the cockpit, as they would create structural weaknesses. I looked about the cabin and found that, despite their mirth at my expense, Team Three was ready for action. They were also deeply troubled by the mystery of our mission, perhaps even frightened.

Fear gnawed at my belly, as well. To keep everyone's nerves steady, I pulled rank and demanded everyone give me a verbal inventory of their equipment. There was some grumbling, but I think they were grateful for the distraction.

"Commander Sk'lar."

I glanced up the aisle to the cockpit.

"What is it, Corporal?"

"I—you'd better come and take a look yourself, sir."

After unbuckling my crash webbing, I carefully made my way up the aisle to lean on his seat, peering intently out the cockpit windshield.

At first, all I noticed were the squat, knobby trees flashing past below. The wind generated by our passage seemed to be making the limbs dance about wildly. Then I realized that the kodanos were locked in combat with the serpentine vines we'd come to recognize as the Puppet Master's signature.

"What are we looking at, Corporal?"

"I'd say the trees are fighting the PM's vines, sir."

"Yes, but why? Doesn't he control most of the vegetation?"

"I don't know, sir. I fly the ship."

Grunting, I quickly stepped back to the cabin and briefed my team and Rouhr on the situation.

"I'm not sure how or why, but the Puppet Master seems to be engaged in conflict with sorvuc and kodanos trees. Those will be our targets. Keep your bursts short and accurate; we still don't know how much destroying the PM's vines will affect the overall organism, and a lot of scientist-types think that if the PM dies, the planet dies. Understand?"

Heads nodded, and Navat let out a loud whoop that I took for an assent.

"Aaah!" I doubled over suddenly, hands on my head. There was a loud buzzing that seemed to be coming from inside my skull. Then my comm implant activated and I heard a synthesized voice.

The Children do not heed my call. I sought to renew. They destroy.

"What's wrong, Commander?"

I waved off Rouhr's ministrations.

"Nothing. I think the Puppet Master has patched himself—itself—into my comm implant, but what he's saying doesn't make any sense."

"Try to understand, Commander. It's probably important. The Puppet Master has contacted me in the past. He is contacting you now. I believe it's important to know why."

"Right." I cleared my throat. "Ah, Puppet Master, are you there?"

A foolish name created by a singular entity. I am vines. Vines are I. Sought to restore that which was lost. The Children are angry. They will not heed.

"So, ah, do you want us to help? And shouldn't you contact the general?"

You all are unique to me. But in times of stress, I reach out to the closest of you that I can.

A few seconds of silence, then— *Also, yes. Assistance is appreciated.*

"Corporal, take us down between this melee and the *Aurora.*"

"Sir?"

"Just do it." I turned to my team. "This is it. Tyehn, Navat, you're on point. Make those trees hurt. Rokul, Takar, and Jalok, you take left flank. Cazak, Zarik, and I will take right. General, would you be so good as to guard our six?"

"It's your rodeo, Sk'lar."

"Sir?"

"A Terran expression. I'm ready to fight."

The craft settled hard on the ground, bouncing us about a bit, but we were up and ready to move down the ramp within seconds.

Tyehn and Navat wielded automatic belt-fed rail guns. The projectiles were slivers of metal, but when they stepped out into the forest and pulled their respective triggers, what looked like pulses of light shot from the barrels.

A nearby sorvuc exploded into gooey kindling. My point men cleared a semi-circle around the ramp while the rest of us disembarked.

I could hear weapons firing from behind me, and I hoped Rokul and his team were able to keep their side clear. Cazak and Zarik were paired with me. Implants in my torso increased the production of stress hormone, increasing my reaction speed and accuracy, but at the expense of raising my blood pressure to moderately high levels. I lined up a shot with my automatic slug thrower. The explosive bullets it fired were ideal for taking down kodanos and the nasty little winged talusians that dwelled within them.

Cochlear implants deadened the nerves in my ear drum, so I didn't go deaf from all the weapons fire. Slowly but surely, we tore a swath through the living and hostile forest.

Alright, the forest here was always hostile, but this was up to new levels.

It was next to impossible not to hit the Puppet Master's vines, but I noticed that my team was at least trying to limit their fire to the trees.

Jalok took a burst of green venom from a sorvuc tree on the arm and went down. His scales and light armor should take care of the toxins, but he was still vulnerable.

I reached down and snagged his good arm, then half dragged him with one hand while firing wildly with my other. Fortunately, explosive ammo meant that I could shoot at the ground and still hit our enemies.

We finally sundered the last of the walking trees, and I did a quick check on my team. Except for Jalok, no one had been injured.

"That's the last of them, General. What's our next move?"

His eyes narrowed, and he looked off over the battlefield toward the *village*.

"Now we go see Fen and hope that she finally has some answers for us."

PHRYNE

Usually when I walked to work, my head was filled with plans and tasks that needed to be completed that today. Today, my thoughts were only of Sk'lar.

Could he be any more perfect?

He was off on a mission, and while a tiny part of me was worried, I knew he'd be fine. He was a kick-ass, hot as hell, alien warrior. Of course he'd be fine.

The fact that thoughts of him were flitting through my head in the first place spoke volumes.

He'd given me my first taste of what true intimacy was supposed to feel like.

And I liked it. I liked *him*.

Somehow, he'd managed to do it without making me feel cornered or trapped, like most relationships had made me feel. Last night meant something, no question. Yet I didn't feel any kind of pressure to define what we were.

I cared about him. He cared about me. That was that.

I could work with that.

Unfortunately, I had to stop thinking about Sk'lar, Sk'lar's body, and Sk'lar in bed.

I approached my building.

Out of habit, I glanced behind me. I didn't expect to see anything, but today I saw an unusual number of people watching me.

On a hunch, I walked past my building and kept going. Periodically checking over my shoulder, I saw that a handful of civilians were following me.

But why?

Something wasn't right.

I cut through an alley and made my way back to the front of my building. Some of my shadows picked up the pace to stay on my trail. Others anticipated my movements and returned to the front of my building before me. I wondered if my attacker was among them.

"Lock the doors," I instructed as soon as I entered the building. "Full lockdown. Something's up."

"Ma'am." Skit appeared at my side.

"Get your partner. I want one of you patrolling the

inside of this building for anything suspicious. You see something, you say something. The other needs to scramble a security unit to patrol the perimeter from a safe vantage point. I don't care who does what. Get it done."

"Yes, ma'am." Skit sped off without hesitating.

"Which strike team can be available immediately?" I called into my radio.

"Strike Team Two standing by," Karzin answered instantly.

"Spread your team out through the levels. Be on high alert, but don't look suspicious."

"Is something wrong?"

"I think so. Do you have a good tech person on your team?"

"Yes, ma'am."

"Get them into the mainframe. If they find anything unusual with the records from last night up until right now, have them contact me immediately."

"Yes, ma'am."

Karzin clicked off. I walked briskly to the stairwell entrance. I wasn't keen on getting into the elevators right now.

When I was nearly to the second-floor landing, someone burst through the stairway entrance and barreled down the stairs, nearly knocking me over.

"Don't go up there!" She was crying. Her makeup

ran down her face in murky tracks. "He's got a gun! He's going to kill someone."

I moved past the terrified woman. The second floor was filled with people crouched on the floor, trembling and trying to move under cover. An intern, barely old enough to grow a mustache, pointed towards Vidia's office with a shaking hand. I nodded my thanks and drew my weapon.

I heard nothing to suggest a fight. A stone of dread sank to the pit of my stomach as I approached Vidia's office. I braced myself for the worst, for seeing her dead on the floor in a puddle of her own blood.

I pressed my back against the wall beside her office door and listened, just in case.

"Malkin, listen to me," came Vidia's voice. I froze. Malkin? He was on my alpha team. I'd hand selected him and trained him myself.

"I'm done listening!" Malkin shouted.

The door to Vidia's office was closed, but not latched. I could bump it open without alerting Malkin, assuming his back was to the door. I moved slowly, moving the door open slowly with my foot.

As I suspected, he had his back to me. Vidia stood behind her desk with her hands up. Though I couldn't see it for myself, I suspected Malkin had a weapon.

Where the hell was General Rouhr?

"My wife was torn to pieces in front of me when those bug-things attacked," he said.

"I know, Malkin," Vidia replied. "Your wife, Lindette, was an amazing woman. I grieve for her, too."

"You have no idea what I'm going through!" Malkin shouted.

"You're right," Vidia said quickly.

If she noticed me, she didn't give anything away.

"Do you want to know how my daughter died?" Malkin asked.

I felt a pang in my heart. Malkin was mad with grief. He didn't wait for Vidia to answer.

"She was crushed to death under a collapsing building when that plant attacked the city. She was only nineteen!"

"I'm so sorry." Tears welled up in Vidia's eyes.

"You're sorry? If you're so sorry, why are you partnering up with the monsters that took my family from me?" Malkin demanded.

"We have to band together to undo the damage-"

"Spare me that bullshit!" Malkin roared. "You're climbing into bed with an abomination every night. You are an affront to humanity and I won't let you stain our race any longer."

I closed the space between me and Malkin. He didn't realize I was there until the tip of my blaster pressed into the base of his head.

"I won't shoot if you won't."

"Here to save the alien-lover, huh?" Malkin laughed dryly.

"I'm here to stop you from becoming a murderer. Do you really want that on your conscience? I know you, Malkin. You're better than this."

"My life is already over. I just want to do some good before I'm done."

"Then lower your weapon," I urged.

"And allow my planet to fall into the hands of someone who will sell us out to aliens in a heartbeat? Never."

His finger moved for the trigger. I lifted both hands and brought the butt of my blaster down hard on the tenderest point in his shoulder. The pain made him drop his blaster. I pulled him back and rushed forward in an attempt to kick the blaster out of reach, but he elbowed me in the stomach.

I doubled over as the air rushed out of my lungs.

"Vidia, get out of here," I wheezed. "Get the general."

"The general isn't here," Malkin laughed. No wonder he'd chosen now to attack.

Vidia made a dash to get by, but Malkin grabbed her around the waist. Vidia thrashed and landed a few well-placed kicks. Malkin slammed her onto her desk.

"It doesn't have to be this way!" she shouted.

Malkin wrapped his hands around her throat. There

was a crazed look in his eyes. There was no humanity left in him.

I slammed into him from the side, but didn't have enough force to make him release Vidia. I grabbed my blaster once more.

"I *will* shoot you," I warned him. It was like I hadn't said anything at all. Vidia's face was beet red.

"Malkin, don't make me kill you!" I shouted.

Vidia writhed against him. His knuckles were white where he squeezed her throat.

I didn't remember pulling the trigger. I didn't remember the sound it made as it fired the beam. I did remember Malkin slumping over on top of Vidia. I remembered Vidia taking in deep gasps of air.

"Phryne," she coughed.

I snapped back into action. I yanked Malkin's body off her and shoved it onto the floor.

"You all right?" I asked.

Vidia nodded as she massaged her throat gently.

"Are you?"

I didn't know how to answer that.

"Vidia!" Karzin burst into the office.

"I'm fine," she insisted, even though she was shaking all over.

"Who is this?" he demanded.

"Disgruntled employee," I answered. "I think the anti-alien radicals got to him."

"If they got to one of our own, who knows how many more they've infected with their poisonous mindset," Karzin growled. "I have half a mind to round all of the radicals up and execute them."

"That wouldn't help anything," Vidia replied.

"I know. But it'd make me feel better," Karzin grumbled.

"Me, too," I agreed. "I really didn't want to kill him."

"You'd have rather spared him?"

"I would've preferred to take him in for questioning. He could've given us names of others who shared his mindset. There could be other people in this building right now prepared to attempt what he just did."

"Was he acting out of the ordinary recently?" Karzin asked.

"He's been working with me for three years," I said. "He didn't show any signs of doing something like this."

"The anti-alien radicals must've gotten to him recently," Karzin surmised.

"Or he simply lost control of his grief," Vidia offered.

"The fact that we don't know for certain is a problem," I said. "We have to screen every employee now. Anyone with even the tiniest hint of suspicious activity has to go. We're compromised."

"I think that's the best course of action," Karzin agreed. "We can't take any more risks."

"I'll get to work on a screening protocol and-"

Shots rang out, followed by a smattering of screams.

Radio chatter exploded in my earpiece. Karzin and I reached for our handsets at the same time.

"What's going on?" Karzin demanded, his voice roaring both beside me and through my earpiece.

"We're under attack," One of Karzin's team members shouted back. "Radicals are inside the building and they have us surrounded. All exit points are under radical control."

"Shit," I swore. "Try to get someone to guard the armory. We don't want the radicals gaining access to our weapons. Someone needs to sweep the floors and get all non-combat-trained personal somewhere safe."

"Yes, ma'am."

I bent down and retrieved Malkin's blaster from beside his body.

"Get to one of the safe rooms, Vidia," I instructed.

"Like hell, I will." Vidia set her jaw.

"I know you're fully capable of kicking ass, but if something happens to you, the radicals win."

"She's right," Karzin agreed. "Get somewhere safe. We'll take it from here. General Rouhr will skin me if anything happens to you."

"Fine," Vidia reluctantly agreed. "Just don't die, okay? Either of you."

"We'll do our best." I gave her a reassuring smile before nodding to Karzin.

Together, we stepped out of Vidia's office, ready for battle.

I should've been coming up with attack plans, but only one thought was prominent in my head at the moment. Where the hell was Sk'lar?

SK'LAR

"Easy on the landing," Cazak snarled at Tyehn as the shuttle came down to land.

"Hey, don't blame me for turbulence," Tyehn snapped back in defense. "I don't have control of the wind."

"Yeah, well, you should..."

"Shut up, both of you," I snapped at them as we touched down. "We're all on edge because of the fight with the trees, but this is getting stupid. You know he can't control turbulence, Cazak."

"You're right," he said before turning to Tyehn. "My apologies. I'm just," he ran his hand over his head. "Boss is right, I'm a bit on edge."

"No worries," Tyehn said.

"Aww," Navat started. "Now that you two ladies are

done, we're on the ground. Can we do this, already? The general's getting antsy."

He wasn't exactly right about that, because Rouhr looked amused by our interactions, but he was known for his ability to show calm in even the most stressful situations. He could be antsy, as Navat said, and just not showing it.

"Navat's right," I said before Cazak or Tyehn could retaliate. "Let's go. Fen's waiting for us." Tyehn pushed the button to open the bay door and we all squinted as the bright light shone into the shuttle. Rouhr led the way out the door. I brought up the rear, making sure Tyehn and Cazak weren't acting like fools on the way out.

Rouhr led us to Fen's home, where she both worked and slept. Then again, I wasn't sure if I had ever seen a Urai sleep. I actually wondered about it. I knew they were all locked up in stasis when the ship crashed here, so they were technically sleeping then, but I don't know if I've ever seen any of them sleep since.

To be honest, this would be the fourth time I'd been inside Fen's home, and I didn't remember ever seeing a bedroom. She had a small kitchen, and a bathroom— still a terrible name the humans had come up with for where to relieve yourself, but then again, humans were odd—as well as a sitting room where you could relax and enjoy yourself.

She also had the office that seemed to take up most of the home, which had been made up of a combination of *Aurora* parts and native materials.

"My friends," Fen said as we entered her home, "thank you for coming. I know it was an inconvenience."

"A bit of one," Rouhr said. "I would like to know why we weren't allowed to use the rift."

"I understand," Fen replied as she indicated the large table in the center of the room. "If you would all please sit, I will explain and show you something."

We all took seats around the table as two other Urai brought out a portable viewscreen and Fen did something with her computer. Once the viewscreen was connected to her computer, we watched as she clicked through some things before putting up what looked like four videos.

"My friends," Fen said as she moved to the viewscreen. As she tapped the screen and made one of the videos take up the entirety of it, she turned to us. "There are some things that I wish to show you in order to better explain what I believe is happening with the humans of this planet, and why I would not open a rift for you." She nodded at Rouhr as she said the last part. "Please watch carefully."

She played the video and we watched as a rift opened. It looked like a typical rift, bright yellow, orange, and white colors nearly blinding our eyes as we watched a Urai step through it to the other side, then step back through.

"What you have just watched is a typical rift opening between here and Glymna before the extermination of the Xathi," Fen explained. "Did you notice anything particular about that rift?"

None of us answered for a moment, then Rouhr cleared his throat. "It looked like a standard rift with the bright colors nearly blinding us, the two or three steps everyone takes inside it, then the exit. It always looks like a tear in space to me."

Fen nodded. "That's exactly what the rift is. It is a tear in space. You see, what a rift does, is it folds space and brings two points together."

"Wait a minute," Jalok cut in. "What do you mean it 'folds space'?"

"Friend Jalok," Fen nodded to him. "If you could imagine the universe as a piece of paper, infinitely long in any direction."

"Okay. I guess," Jalok said. "So, you're going to say that the rift folds the universe like I can fold a piece of paper?"

"To a point, yes."

"But that makes no sense," Jalok argued. "If I fold a piece a paper, then both sides of that paper are either touching or really close to touching. If you're folding space with the rift device, then how come only a single point connects to the other side of space?"

"That is a valid question," Fen responded. "When the rift folds space, it only folds the two connection points to one another. However, it does not connect the two points to one another, that is why you must walk through the rift before arriving on the other side."

Jalok opened his mouth, but Rouhr held up his hand to stop him. "Okay. But, what does all of that have to do with you not opening a rift for us and what's happening with the humans?"

"Patience, General," Fen answered. "The next video was what I wanted to show you." She minimized the first video, then brought up the second one. "This second video is of a rift opening taken a couple of days ago." She pressed the play button and we watched. Rouhr shot forward in his chair, but I wasn't sure what he was looking at. It looked like a rift to me, just like all the others. Perhaps the edges looked a little different, but I've never paid attention to each individual rift I've gone through.

"What are you showing us, Lady Fen?" I asked.

"Perhaps once more," she said. She replayed the video and I looked again.

It looked like a tear in space, like all rifts do. The rich blue, green, and purple lighting was hard to see through. I could see the other side of the— "Oh, skrell," I said out loud. "What the rek?"

"You see it, don't you?" Fen said.

Everyone looked at me, Fen looked pleased, Rouhr looked upset, the others looked lost. Suddenly, Tyehn's eyes went wide and he twisted his head to look at the screen again. "What colors were the rift last time?"

Each of them gave me a different answer, which was typical whenever we used the rift. Everyone always described it differently.

"Okay, what are the colors on that video?"

Each one of them said "Blue, green, and purple." They all looked at one another, then back at me.

"That's right," I said with a nod. "We've never seen the same colors, in the same order, at the same time before."

"That's not all," Rouhr said. "The first video showed that the rift looked like a tear in the fabric of space, but it looked like a tear that was made with a knife, you know?"

We all nodded.

"This time, this tear looks like something just reached out and ripped it apart," Rouhr said. We all looked at the screen and studied the rift. Fen put the picture of the other rift from the earlier video up via split-screen and we could see it. The original rift looked as though someone had cut space, then ripped it open.

The second rift was jagged and broken, as if someone had grabbed a cloth between two hands and pulled apart as hard as they could.

"That is correct," Fen said. "The rifts have changed. The space between the openings, that is an unknown space that exists outside the known boundaries of the universe. I believe that something has come out of that space and entered our own."

"But what?" Tyehn asked before any of the rest of us could.

"I'm not certain," she answered. "However, look at these." She tapped the viewscreen and sent the rift videos away, then brought up brain scans. "These are two separate brain scans from one person. The one on the right is their healthy brain. The one on the left is after they suddenly turned against you."

"How did you manage to get a brain scan for a before and after?" Rouhr asked.

"Dr. Evie Parr is a remarkable person. And she also had remarkable luck. This particular human had come in for a routine check-up after the dome was erected and Evie had conducted a brain scan then. This same person was one of the ones arrested the other day," Fen explained.

"What are we looking for?" Navat asked. "I don't see anything."

"Very good," Fen said. "Look closer, however. Right

here." She pointed at a part of the brain on the left and zoomed it in for us.

"Is that, what is that?" Navat asked.

"That is a parasitic presence within the human brain," Fen answered.

"Show us the other scan," Rouhr ordered.

Fen zoomed in on the same section of the brain as the one on the left. There was nothing there.

"You mean that there's a chance that something came out of the rift and started taking people over?" Rouhr asked.

"Yes, I believe so," Fen answered.

"But how?"

"I wish I knew," Fen said. "It is something that I must continue to study."

"Then we need to—" Rouhr started saying before all of our comms erupted in alarm. Rouhr clicked on his, listened for a few seconds, then jumped to his feet. "The offices are under attack. We need to leave, *now*."

PHRYNE

"Have we gotten a head count yet?" I spoke into the comm.

I'd taken cover behind an overturned desk. This was the first chance I'd had to get information from everyone since the first shots went off. It'd been total chaos ever since. I went down to the first floor to find madness. The gates at the front had been breached, with at least two dozen radicals pouring into the lobby, and more standing by. With two out of three strike teams gone and the majority of the ground teams out patrolling, we were quickly outnumbered and in retreat to more defensible positions.

"Of the radicals or of us?" Iq'her of Strike Team Two called back.

"Radicals."

"Enough to overrun the first floor and cut off all exits." As if I didn't already know that.

"They're aggressive," Karzin joined in. "They intend to kill. Should we switch to lethal rounds?"

"Not yet." As much as I wanted to vaporize every single person who'd threatened me and mine, the radicals were more valuable to us alive. "Tranq rounds, paralysis rounds, and sleeper gas only."

"Yes, ma'am."

"They're fighting to get to the stairwell," Rokul called in. "Some ground team members are covering the elevators."

"Someone needs to cut power to the elevators," I ordered.

"On it."

"I need a status update." General Rouhr's voice sounded muffled. He must've been using a comm system built into an aerial unit.

"The first floor is overrun. We're trying to get everyone up to the second floor. We're cutting power to the elevators. The radicals will have to take the stairs and bottleneck themselves," I reported back.

"Where's Vidia?"

"She was making her way to one of the safe rooms when I last saw her."

"I saw her enter the safe room unscathed," Sylor reported.

General Rouhr loosed a sigh of relief.

"Does anyone have eyes on Sk'lar?" I couldn't help but ask.

"Strike Team Three is out at *Aurora* village with me. They've been notified of the situation," General Rouhr replied. "I jumped in an aerial unit the second I heard about the attack. They shouldn't be far behind me."

"Still no rift access?"

"Negative."

"Damn it. What about Strike Team One?" I asked.

"Negative, as well. They're in Glymna."

I bit my tongue so I wouldn't shout. Why the hell was our team so scattered when security threats were so prevalent? At least most of my Alpha team was here. I didn't have to worry about being in constant communication with them. They were trained to deal with things like this. Granted, none of us ever thought this would happen.

I should check on Tona and Skit after this. They were far from incompetent, but they weren't trained by me. They wouldn't automatically know how to fit into our operations.

"Power's cut to the elevators."

"Fall back from the elevators," Karzin barked. "Get all personnel to the second floor."

"Yes, sir."

"They're going to have to fight through a lot of

radicals to get to the stairwell," Iq'her warned. "Might be a good time to switch to lethal rounds."

"Not yet," General Rouhr ordered. "If this turns into a massacre, the radicals still win."

He was right. If we used lethal force, that would only reinforce the idea that the aliens were out to harm humans.

"Force them to crowd into the stairwell," I said. "Limit how many can attack at once."

Before anyone could reply to me, I clicked to my team's personal frequency.

"Tona. Skit. One of you come in," I barked.

"Ma'am." I think it was Tona.

"Location?"

"Second floor, top of the stairwell," he replied.

"Where's Skit?"

"Moving non-combat-trained personnel into the safe rooms."

"Excellent. Are you alone?"

"No, I'm with the other members of your team."

"Great. I need you to do something for me."

Footsteps skittered past me. I carefully peeked over the desk. Two radicals moved through the room, probably to join the others.

"Stand by, Tona."

I leaped up and fired a sleeper round at the radicals' backs. One quickly succumbed to the airborne tranq gas. The other was more resilient. He turned, and with a crazed look in his eyes, charged at me.

He was bigger and stronger than I, but he was untrained in combat. All he knew how to do was throw punches. I ducked and evaded with ease before nailing him right in a pressure point. He slumped into unconsciousness at my feet.

I tapped the grip of my blaster, fighting the urge to blow a hole through his forehead.

"Ma'am?" Tona's voice came through the earpiece.

"Yes, I'm here. I need you to go to the control room and call back the city patrol teams. Tell them to prepare for a fight, but to avoid killing if they can."

"Yes, ma'am."

I clicked back to the general channel.

"Is the first floor clear?" General Rouhr asked.

"Can't say for sure," Karzin asked.

"I'm still down here," I said. "I don't see any other allies."

"Get up here when you can. We need all the help we can get," Karzin said.

With the elevators shut down and the stairwell clogged with idiots who'd like to kill me, I needed an alternate plan. I visualized the emergency exits. All the ones leading to the street were no doubt clogged with waiting radicals.

There were the remains of an old fire escape still

attached to the building, but that was old even before the Xathi attacked. Still, it was better than nothing. If I remembered correctly, the ladder was positioned on the southeast side of the building.

I crept over to the window. Once I was certain none of the radicals were waiting on this side of the building, I opened it.

The ladder was only half unfurled. I climbed out the window and stood on the sill for extra height. With a grunt, I leaped from the sill, barely grasping the bottom rung of the ladder. I hauled myself up. The ladder was so rusted I worried it wouldn't hold my weight, but somehow it did.

Once safely on the landing of the fire escape, I kicked at the ladder until it broke off. If I figured this out, one of the radicals would figure it out eventually. I couldn't risk being followed up here.

I saw the backs of my colleagues through the second floor window. I knocked, startling them.

Karzin opened the window for me.

"You could've warned us," he said.

"I didn't want anyone overhearing my plan. Status?"

"Just like you predicted, the radicals bottle-headed themselves."

"Bottlenecked," I corrected with a smirk.

"Someone had the good sense to bring extra ammo up from the armory. We're rotating." Karzin gestured to the group of soldiers and security officers surrounding the stairwell door. "I'm reloading my weapons and then I'll relieve someone who's running low."

"Fantastic." The knot of tension in my chest released. "The radicals will run out of energy or out of ammo sooner or later. Think we can hold out?"

"Reinforcements will be here in ten minutes," Tona announced. "We can definitely hold out."

"Good work," I nodded to him.

"Thank you, ma'am. That means a lot."

"Don't get sentimental on me yet, solider. We haven't won this fight."

"Yes, ma'am."

I gave Tona a pat on the shoulder before making my way to the stairwell entry. Two of my team members, Mekinna and Cyrus, stood to attention briefly before each launched a sleeper grenade down into the stairwell. A few yards ahead of them, strike team members and officers held the radicals at bay with shields surrounded by energy fields.

"Status report?"

"They're losing energy," Cyrus said. "The sleeper gas is most effective."

"Do we know what their reload capabilities are?"

"Most of them have extra rounds in their pockets, but they're burning through them fast."

"Any casualties on our part?"

"A few grazes. I suspect the radicals are using homemade rounds. They're incapable of puncturing our armor," Mekinna reported.

"That's a relief."

"There's something odd about the radicals," Cyrus said as he launched another grenade. Violet-colored gas exploded in the center of the cluster. Some radicals fell back in a coughing fit, others pushed forward despite their sloppy movements.

"Something in their eyes?" I guessed.

"Affirmative," Mekinna said. "They appear to be under the influence of the same substance that the radicals at the riot were under."

"Not surprising."

A radical forced himself through two of the shields, despite the electric pulses shooting through him from the energy fields. His eyes gleamed in an inhuman way. I lifted my weapon and sent a tranq dart into his neck. He collapsed and slipped down the stairs, taking out several others as he fell.

"Reinforcements are here," Tona reported through the radio.

"Remind them to avoid lethal force," I warned. "I want to question as many of these brutes as possible."

"Yes, ma'am."

The radicals farthest from the second floor turned their attention to face the onslaught coming from behind them. Between the unfaltering forces at the top of the stairs and the wave of fresh forces below, the radicals soon found themselves outmatched.

"They're retreating," I barked into the radio. "Move forward and restrain whoever you can catch."

Within moments, the sound of weapons firing echoed through the first floor.

"They still have ammo," Karzin reported. "They must've saved some rounds for their retreat."

"Proceed with caution," I advised.

"They're determined not to leave anyone behind," Karzin reported after a few moments.

"How many captives are we looking at?"

"None." Karzin was frustrated. "They clearly had an extraction plan. They're using ammo they didn't use during the actual attack."

"What kind of ammo?"

"Looks like some kind of homemade casing containing jagged bits of shrapnel," Karzin said. "They tore the officers' armor to shreds."

"Any deaths?"

"One male took a bad hit in the chest. If we get him to Evie, she'll probably be able to help him."

"Let the radicals go," I instructed. "Don't let anyone put themselves at risk. It's not worth it."

"Yes, ma'am."

Well, that was disappointing. As I returned to the

first floor, I wondered why the radicals would bring such intense ammo to only use it while retreating. Clearly, they all knew something that was more important for them to keep secret.

As much as I wanted captives to pump for information, I wasn't going to call this a loss. We'd held our own and driven the radicals out. Between one step and the next, exhaustion hit me as the adrenaline drained out of me. I glanced at the timepiece on the wall. The radicals had attacked two hours ago.

I slumped down on a broken chair and took a breath.

"Strike Team Three has returned," someone called through the radio. I perked up from my seat just as Sk'lar and his team entered the first-floor lobby.

"What'd I miss?" he asked with a grin.

"One hell of a party."

SK'LAR

Placid, calm on the outside, belly roiling with anxiety on the inside, I wondered if anyone else at this emergency meeting felt as out of their element as I did.

Here on the top floor of the Nyheim official building, we were treated to a magnificent view of the setting sun as it lent dying scarlet light to the city. Everything seemed safe and tranquil, belying the recent chaos which had rocked this metropolis.

I had grown used to General Rouhr, and Vidia, and of course I didn't feel uncomfortable around Phryne, but there were some heavyweights here.

Vrehx and Karzin sat with almost bored expressions, as if waiting for the bean counters and bureaucrats to hurry up and decide who should get shot.

Dr. Parr was here, as well, lending her expertise to the discussion. A worried frown wrinkled her otherwise attractive face. Given recent events, I couldn't blame her one bit for feeling upset. Tona and Skit, two of Nyheim's security personnel, stood a few feet behind her chair.

Thribb and Tyehn sat flanking me, because Thribb was our science guy and I was hoping Tyehn's own scientific background might offer some unique insight. I guess I also felt that, somehow, the entourage made me seem less unimportant.

Vidia stood up, drained half a glass of what I assumed to be water, and took in the whole room with her gaze.

"Let's cut to the chase. Things are going to hell in a handbasket—don't roll your eyes, Rouhr, it's not the most obscure human phrase—and we need to pull together and fix this mess. First up is the Election. Thoughts?"

Dr. Parr was the first to speak.

"We'll have to suspend the elections. With all of the chaos, there's no way that we can possibly ensure they will be both secure and fair."

Rouhr glared at her, and his mouth opened and

closed several times. When he finally spoke up, it was as if he'd barely contained his incredulity.

"You would have us suspend the elections and give even more ammunition to the anti-alien propaganda machine?" he asked. "Are you mad?"

"But Dashiell just straight-up called us traitors," she said.

Karzin shook his head and eyed Parr as if she'd lost her mind as she continued, "He was ranting and raving like a lunatic. There's no way such a man is a viable or worthy candidate."

"You're not looking at the big picture," another voice interjected.

We all turned to Phryne as she stood up and put her arms akimbo.

"What General Rouhr is getting at is this; if we kick Dashiell out of the election, then the anti-alienists will have a lightning rod with which to draw others to their cause. As vile as the man is, as much as I *do not* agree with his views on non-humans, we have to let him run."

Everyone fell silent at that. Rouhr didn't gloat that his point had been made, because this wasn't the type of victory you celebrated. At length, I tapped on the table to get everyone's attention.

"The election matter is settled, though not to anyone's liking." Nods around the table indicated assent. "Moving on to our next order of business. Fen believes that we may be dealing with as yet unseen hostile forces, who are affecting the very minds of not only humans, but the native flora and fauna as well."

"And she thinks that the rifts are to blame." We all turned to Dr. Parr. "I'm not Fen, by a long shot, but her research seems solid. We're working on a countermeasure, but with so little data to go on, I'm afraid we're moving at a snail's pace."

"Great." Phryne slammed her fist on the table, startling several people. "So that's two problems we can do exactly jack and rek about."

I had to smile at the way she casually dropped K'veri dialect into her speech.

"Sk'lar." I looked up to meet Rouhr's somber gaze. "I read your after-action report on the engagement with the, shall we call them possessed, tree-like species and the Puppet Master's tendrils. It concurs with what I saw and I wanted to commend you on a job well done."

"Thank you, sir." Now I felt really out of place, like everyone was looking at me. I decided to concentrate on Phryne. There was a light in her lovely eyes, a kind of mischief that said she was enjoying my discomfort to a degree. I also detected that particular glint which indicated she wanted to be intimate again. Soon.

"If the Puppet Master is losing control over his 'children,' we should draft plans on what to do if the trees get violent again."

"Sir." Everyone faced me once again. "I believe both you and Vidia should be assigned additional security details, for now until the election is over, at least."

"Agreed." General Rouhr took in the room and sighed. "I know things look bleak right now, but we've survived worse. We've beaten off the Xathi. We can take it. Meeting adjourned."

Everyone filtered out of the chamber, and I wound up riding an elevator with Phryne. She leaned against the opposite wall, crossed her arms, and gave me a meaningful, smoldering look.

As soon as the doors shut, she rushed to me, grabbing me in a fierce embrace. We kissed, hands clutching at each other's bodies as if we couldn't be close enough to satisfy our urges. I once heard an old K'ver soldier claim that there was no better aphrodisiac than fear. Maybe he was right, or maybe we were just that smitten with each other.

The taste of Phryne's mouth drove me wild, and my body responded. A smile spread over her face when she felt my growing erection. She leaped up, wrapping her legs around my hips, and started grinding herself into me while we explored and probed with lips and tongues.

"Ah, I'll take the next one."

We turned our heads, gaping in shock at the sight of Dr. Parr and General Rouhr standing in the doorway. I wondered how long they had been standing there. Rouhr had a gentle grin on his face as the doors shut, while Dr. Parr was beaming at us with her gaze.

Phryne and I laughed, and she dropped her feet back to the floor. I grinned down at her.

"Clearly, I need to work off this pent-up energy," she gasped.

I needed much, much more than that. But working off energy would do. For a start.

"So, to your place, then?"

"No."

"What?"

"Your place is closer."

"Very well." I rubbed my thumb over her freckled cheek and she sighed softly. "I'm afraid my room is not very big."

"Does it have a bed?"

"Yes."

"Then it will do, won't it?"

After an admittedly rushed stroll to my apartment complex, we made it all the way up to my front door before mauling one another. We stumbled inside my flat, and I was barely able to snag the door with my toe and shut it before she threw me onto my mattress.

"Nice place." She was not even looking at my meager dwelling, which consisted of a ten-foot square kitchen area, a commode, and a shower, all in one room. There's also an IDM center—Implant Diagnostic and Maintenance—which resembled a large metal chair with an attached monitor.

"Let me show you around."

I grabbed her and tossed her onto the mattress beneath me. She laughed, caressing my cheek as I smiled down at her. Phryne was gorgeous, fierce, but playful at the same time. Her strange edges seemed to fit well with my own. I began to kiss her on the neck, and she rolled her head backward. Then she spotted the IDM chair for the first time.

"No way."

She squirmed out from under me, causing me to groan in frustration. I smiled ruefully at her naked body as she sauntered with sinuous grace over to the imposing seat.

"Is this a sex thing? I didn't know you K'ver were so kinky."

Laughing, I rose naked from the bed and came over to her side. I sat in the chair, automatically activating its systems. Lines of blue light lit up all over the seat and synched with the pieces of circuitry visible on my skin.

"What in the world?" Phryne gaped as a computer rendered image of my circulatory and endocrine system showed up on the screen. My implants were also visible, with readouts next to each. "Is that what's inside you?"

"Yes. This chair allows me to monitor and perform simple repairs on my implants and cyberware. All K'ver with more than five implants have one."

"Hmm." She tapped the screen. "Looks like a lot of blood is rushing down here for some reason."

She wriggled her bottom, then pointedly strutted over in front of me. Phryne leapt into my naked lap, kissing my neck and nuzzling against me.

"My body's tingling."

"Curious." I looked past her to see the monitor, where her systems were also on display. "The chair has synched to your system, as well. I always assumed it only worked on K'ver."

"Do you really want to talk tech right now?" Phryne reached down and grabbed my swollen cock firmly. "Or do you want to fuck?"

I wanted to do much more than that. Phryne's scent, her taste, her voice, were becoming as much a part of me as my own circuitry.

But my strong, tough lady didn't want to hear that. Not yet.

So for now, I kissed her by way of an answer. Phryne lifted up on her haunches and guided the head of my cock between her wide open, dripping wet pussy lips. Micron by micron, she forced herself down my wide shaft until she was seated in my lap. We gasped in unison as I became fully sheathed in her. Her pussy muscles tensed up around my cock, squeezing me with surprising strength.

"You like that?" Her voice was husky in my ear.

"Yes..." I groaned, striving to hold back longer. I'd barely been in her a minute.

Phryne swiveled her hips, moving her body like the sea in a storm. I reached up and cupped both of her breasts, kneading her pliant flesh and using my handhold to control her body's movements to a degree.

She gasped and clasped her hands around my wrists, but didn't try to change my grip. If anything, she pressed my palms down more firmly onto her soft breasts.

I lowered my head to her neck, tasting and nipping at her skin, feeling her pulse race with every movement as I drove into her.

"Oh god, oh god, your cock feels so good inside me." Her eyes squeezed shut, and she fell backward, body arching in a lovely way that had the side effect of allowing me to thrust even deeper into her tight heat.

Moving my hand to her hip, I pulled her tighter to me, shifting the control of our movements until I drove into her, even harder and deeper with each pounding thrust, until she shattered in my grip.

Every moan, every expression she made as she fell over the edge of orgasm again and again spurred me on, until, with a roar, I watched our fused bodies lighting up on the monitor as we came in unison.

At last, I pulled her back up into my lap and held her in my arms. We remained that way for a time as our breathing slowed. I remained inside her until our hearts calmed, and we still cuddled in the chair long after the sun had sunk below the horizon.

PHRYNE

S k'lar took up much of my headspace as I walked to work.

Too much.

Thinking about him was becoming part of my morning ritual. Sleeping with him was also becoming part of my ritual.

The day the radicals tried to take over the building, I walked into work feeling thrilled about the step forward I had taken with Sk'lar.

We'd reached a new level of intimacy that day. I'd taken it in stride, for someone with intimacy issues.

But when he strode into the lobby after the radicals ran off, I felt something in my chest. My first instinct was to run into his arms. That wasn't part of our arrangement.

Our arrangement was that we didn't have an arrangement, right?

No strings.

So why did I feel a pull?

I couldn't allow myself to get caught up in the feelings trap. The fact that no feelings were involved was why Sk'lar and I worked.

Upon reflection, it wasn't accurate to say that there were no feelings involved. I liked Sk'lar. He was fun to hang out with, good for a chat, and was able to keep up with me in the bar, in bed, and at work.

A pretty good trifecta. I let him in as a friend and it'd been one of the best decisions I'd made in recent years.

Things weren't complicated with Sk'lar.

Our agreement to keep feelings out of it was for both our benefits. I couldn't jeopardize the friendship I'd built with him because I'd caught feelings.

I had a laundry list of reasons why a no-strings situation was the best way to go about this. Sk'lar had surely added his own reasons to that list.

I stopped walking dead in my tracks.

I couldn't remember any of the reasons Sk'lar gave. Sure, he'd said positive things about our relationship, but never in the context of being friends with benefits.

Oh, my god.

We'd never agreed to be friends with benefits.

I'd just assumed we were.

I looked back on our first conversation when he climbed into my shower. He asked me not to shut him out. What if he meant that in a romantic way? I automatically assumed he meant that in a physical way or a friendship way.

What if, this whole time, Sk'lar was working toward a real relationship with me?

Not once had he pressured me. I'd taken his willingness to allow me to do things my way as a sign of agreement to a no-strings relationship. I never asked him directly.

What the hell was wrong with me?

This was exactly why I didn't enter into relationships. I made assumptions and I didn't talk about my feelings.

I needed to ask Vidia about this.

She was good with relationships.

She was good with people.

Oh god. I wasn't going to talk to my boss about my alien maybe-boyfriend, was I?

We had a meeting to get through first.

Good. That'd stop me from thinking about how I might've misunderstood my relationship with Sk'lar from day one.

"Good morning." Vidia greeted me when I walked into the conference room on the first floor. The fallout from the radial attack had been cleaned up quickly, though the lobby still showed signs of conflict. The stairwell looked like a nightmare. I was glad cleaning wasn't part of my responsibilities anymore. That was the worst part of training.

"Morning," I grumbled.

"What happened?" Vidia had a knowing smile on her face.

"Nothing."

"That's not true. Your skin is dewy and glowing but your face looks like a thundercloud. Those are conflicting signals."

"I'm not signaling anything. Who called this meeting? This is rather last minute." I pushed past the subject of my dewy-yet-stormy face.

"You're not going to like this," Vidia winced.

"Tell me."

"Dashiell Fox."

"Why are we meeting with your opposition? Your suddenly anti-alien opposition, I might add."

"He's suggesting a change in venue for our debate tomorrow."

"Absolutely not. Why'd you agree to meet for such a ridiculous reason?"

"To gather intel. Maybe he'll let slip his reasoning for flipping his campaign upside down and backward while we talk."

"That seems foolishly optimistic."

"Maybe. But I'm very good at reading people."

"Let me call in some extra security. I don't trust inviting an anti-alien champion into our midst."

"General Rouhr already knows. All non-human personnel are on the second floor working or monitoring from the control room. If Fox so much as looks at me funny, Rouhr's ready to take him down a notch."

"Glad to know you've given this some thought," I conceded.

I pushed my earpiece into place and synced up my device with the building's radio network.

"When's Fox meant to arrive?"

"He's in the lobby now," General Rouhr answered me. "Don't let him pull anything with Vidia."

"If I didn't know better, I'd say you don't think she can handle herself," I jested.

"What?" Vidia perked up.

"Don't get me in trouble," General Rouhr chuckled.

The door to the conference room pushed open. An attendant in an all-black suit and black glasses stepped inside. Dashiell Fox followed.

"Dashiell." Vidia stood, beaming, and went to great her competitor. "So good to see you."

"Good to see you, too, dear." Vidia and Fox kissed each other's cheeks twice before Vidia offered him a seat. I gave Vidia a questioning look, to which she simply smiled. The exchange must've been part of the political tango.

"What can I do for you?" Vidia asked.

"I wanted to request that we move tomorrow's debate to a different location."

"Why?" I asked flatly.

"It's scheduled as an indoor event, which greatly limits how many can attend," Fox replied.

"What do you propose instead?" Vidia asked.

"I propose moving the final debate to the East Square, right next to those lovely complexes you've worked so hard to renovate." Fox's smile was too forced. I watched his eyes for any sign of that mad gleam I'd seen on the panel at the bar, but they were clear.

"Do you have a map of said square?" I asked.

"Unfortunately, no," Fox's frown was filled with false apologies. He turned to Vidia. "I assumed you and your staff would have knowledge of the square since your passion projects are located so nearby."

"I assure you, I'm quite familiar with the square," Vidia said.

"Then let's discuss moving the debate," Fox pressed.

As they talked about potential benefits, I pulled out my datapad and searched through the city plans. I pulled up a map of the square and surrounding buildings. No wonder Fox wanted to move the debate there. It was completely unprotected.

There were far too many entry points for my teams to cover, as well as a number of vantage points where a sniper could have a clear shot at any point in the square.

I gave Vidia a weighted look.

"I'm open to your ideas, Dashiell. Would you allow me to talk it over with my team privately?" she asked.

"Of course, my dear." Dashiell smiled but I saw the anger in his eyes. He knew he couldn't deny her request without looking suspicious. I threw him my own sugary-sweet smile as I led Vidia out of the room. We took the elevator to the second floor to ensure we were out of earshot.

"What did you find out?"

"He wants to lure you into a trap in the square," I replied.

"Not surprising. He's being far too nice."

"He's a terrible actor."

"Indeed. What's concerning about the square?"

"Besides entry points we can't control and too many hidey-holes for snipers?"

"Yes, besides that," Vidia joked.

"It could rain that day," I played along. "Tell Fox that you don't agree with moving the debate."

"Oh, sweet Phryne. This is politics. I have to make him think it's his idea not to move the debate in order for him to agree to it." Vidia smiled slyly.

"Can you do that?"

"I'm offended that you had to ask."

"Get to it then. I'll feel much better with that weasel out of our building."

"He's not a weasel. He's a fox."

"Very funny."

We returned to the conference room. Fox and his attendant sat in silence.

"Let me guess, you're going to refuse to move the debate." Fox's smile was anything but friendly.

"I actually like the idea," Vidia replied, throwing me off guard. I tried not to look surprised. I felt sure Vidia had a plan. This was what she was good at, after all.

Fox looked just as surprised as I felt.

"You do?"

"Of course! I want as many people as possible there to hear the debate. It's only fair that they do. Most families don't have a way to watch the broadcast at home."

"That's exactly my reasoning!" Fox replied.

"I just have to make my poor team scramble," Vidia sighed.

"Are they not organized enough to handle a sudden change?"

"That's not the issue," Vidia said. "For an area that large, we'll have to pull out all the stops with security. Perimeter guards, aerial units. I'm sure you understand."

"Of course." Fox reached across the table to put his hand on top of Vidia's. My skin crawled on her behalf. "These are volatile times, after all."

I know a threat when I hear one.

"My poor head of security wanted to use a small team," Vidia hummed with sympathy. "It's much easier on them that way. That's why the indoor venue is preferable for them."

Fox paused.

"I understand," he said slowly. I watched the wheels in his head turn as he fell into Vidia's play.

"I'm sure you do." Vidia nodded. "We're in the home stretch now. You know how it goes. Most campaign resources are spent by now. I'm sure we're both scraping the bottom of the funding barrel."

"Absolutely." Fox patted Vidia's hand. "In that case, forget about changing the venue. I'm sure it'll be better for both of us, anyway."

"Thank you for being so understanding. I couldn't

ask for a more honorable competitor." Vidia bid him goodbye with a flourish. When we were alone in the conference room once more, I turned to her.

"Don't you think you laid it on kind of thick at the end?"

"Of course!" Vidia snorted. "His ego needed it. He's still a man, after all."

SK'LAR

It was the evening of the debate, and we had things cleared. We had security personnel in tight rotations everywhere across the building. Yet, despite all of that, there were still too many places in a building of this size.

The debate was being held in an indoor stadium to accommodate the number of people that had expressed interest in coming. The stadium was large enough to hold a few thousand people, but we were restricting the count to half that, with large monitors temporarily installed outside the stadium for any overflow.

The stadium had been one of the grandest creations the humans had put together before the Xathi war and, aside from some minor structural damage, it had come through the invasion almost unscathed.

But we only had maybe one hundred guards, and too many of them were humans. I trusted them, but with the "switch," as some of them were calling it to represent the people that suddenly changed personalities and allegiances, there were too many opportunities for one of those human guards to suddenly turn.

That was why no one had lethal rounds. We had to take precautions, and one of those was to make sure that non-lethal rounds were loaded into the weapons by the *Vengeance* crew, then handed out to the guards after they were checked to ensure they had not brought another weapon onto the premises.

At each entrance, we had scanners that checked for anything that could be used as a weapon and had them confiscated, with names in order to ensure the return of said item, and a hope that everything would go well.

I walked my patrol, barely listening to the debate. It was going smoothly, Vidia's opponent was playing nice and not repeating any of the diatribe from his television interview. Perhaps his act earlier was simply a ploy in order to garner votes. As they continued their back-and-forth, I turned my concentration to watching the crowd, which was difficult. There were simply too many people and too many possibilities.

I looked up to the podium, not to pay attention to the debate, but to see how Phryne and her team were doing. She still trusted her people, despite having gone through the attack on the offices and one of her own betraying them.

She looked prepared and vigilant standing just off to Vidia's left. Several others of her team were spread out in front of the dais the two candidates were debating on. The other security team was spread out the same, and they were doing their job well.

I was impressed.

As I looked back to Phryne, I started thinking about how well we fit together. I had no illusions about how I'd gotten my command position. I knew I wasn't Rouhr's first choice when he gave it to me, and that the only reason I got it was because I was the only K'ver willing to take the position. I knew I wasn't close to my team and that, while they would do their jobs and we would all sacrifice ourselves for the others, they didn't consider me to be a friend.

Phryne made me forget all of that.

She was unusual, brash, funny, and seemed to know what she wanted and took the steps she needed to get what she wanted. She was to the point and I liked that about her. Yes, it had been tough to deal with her at first, but she had to be hard and tough working as security. If you threw in the inescapable fact that she was security for possibly the most powerful human on the planet, in terms of politics, she had to be extra tough. Yet she did her job without complaint and put everything that she could into it.

That was when she was at work. When she was off duty, she opened up and I found myself looking forward to being around her more off duty than anything. She was unusual when compared to other women, and it was a level of unusualness that appealed to me. I enjoyed playing pool with her, as well as other games. I enjoyed spending time with her talking about the most off-the-wall things. She would tell me about things she used to do as a child, like how she used to climb one of the trees in the park as high as she possibly could, then jumped off into the lake. Or how she would collect unusual looking rocks just because they were different looking. Or how she used to take her neighbor's toys to play with them because her parents didn't want to get her 'boy's toys' and she really wanted to play with them.

While that normally wouldn't be counted as unusual, it was the fact that she was so proud of it all, even now as an adult, that made it cute and weird. It reminded me a lot of my own idiosyncrasies from my youth. I actually still had some of my original augmentations from when I was a child. I had chosen my original augmentations based on their bright colors instead of what they could do for me. I was the child that was never able to keep up physically because I never had the right augmentations, and I didn't care because I enjoyed the colors.

That's what I liked about Phryne. Her unusual fit with my unusual, and I loved it. We also had a relationship that played off one another so well without all the "I love you" moments that the others had. I did love spending time with Phryne, and I knew that there was no one else around that made me feel as good as she did, but we didn't need those sappy moments of expression between us.

We just played off one another perfectly, and that...

A gunshot and a stadium full of screams ripped me from my thoughts and back to reality. A quick scan showed Vidia and Phryne down on the ground, her opponent also down, hiding behind his podium. In the center of the crowd, closest to where I stood, I spotted the shooter. The crowd had spread itself away from the shooter in its panic to get away.

I raised my own rifle and took a shot at the shooter, but someone jostled me as I shot and I missed, striking the ground by his feet. He looked at me as if I was nothing, then, as I raised my rifle to shoot again, he took off running into the crowd.

"Rek," I cursed as I gave chase. It was hard to weave my way through the crowd, as they were all trying to get away from the chaos, ironically creating more chaos in the process.

I shoved my way through the crowd, trying my hardest to keep my eye on the shooter. Thankfully, it wasn't hard to do. The man that had pulled the trigger had bright blonde hair and pale skin, and he stood taller than most of the people in the crowd.

I was knocked off my feet and forced to fight my way back up. My hand was stepped on, someone tripped over me and fell on my back, and I felt a knee strike me in the side of the head, but it didn't feel like a purposeful shot. I somehow managed to get back to my feet, feeling a bit groggy.

I blinked quickly, trying to clear my vision. I looked around, temporarily lost, then found the shooter, standing in the middle of the chaos, staring at me. It was possibly the most unnerving thing I had ever seen. The look in his eyes was, I couldn't describe it, I couldn't understand it. He looked as though he was waiting for me, as though he was wanting me to chase him. Then, his eyes flashed and he turned to run again.

I forced my way through the crowd, and things were beginning to clear, making it easier for me to move. The shooter had made his way through the crowd and was climbing the steps of the stadium seating area. I wasn't far behind, but had to stop as a mother rushed by me with her child in her arms. I finally got through and bounded up the stairs, my superior stride helping me to catch up to the blonde man.

He made the top of the stairs and turned left on the concourse, with me only a few steps behind. He was quick, but I was faster. As he rounded a corner, he took an awkward step that I ignored, and it cost me. I stepped right into a puddle of liquid and I went sprawling, sliding and rolling across the floor as he continued to run away.

I cursed my stupidity, regained my footing, and took off after him again.

I finally caught up to him, already being arrested by Tyehn as Navat and Jalok pointed their weapons at him.

"Go check on Phryne," Navat said. "We have this piece of garbage."

I nodded, glared at the shooter, then made my way down the stairs, bounding down them two or three at a time. At the podium, I could see several members of Phryne's team kneeling next to her as she lay still on the ground.

No! Oh, please, don't let her dead!

I could see the darkening wet spot on her back getting bigger and I raced faster. One of her team looked up as I raced over. "She's still breathing. The bullet hit low, but it doesn't look like it hit anything vital, we hope."

"We've already called for medical," Vidia said, her face calm but her eyes filled with concern, fear, and rage. "They're on their way in now."

All I could do was nod as I knelt next to Phryne, reaching out and grabbing her hand.

Don't die. We have so much to talk about still. Just don't die.

PHRYNE

The first thing I noticed was the smell. I was sleeping in a bed, yet it didn't smell like my place. My thoughts clicked together in slow motion like each one was dipped in wet cement.

All I could focus on was the strange smell. I heard nothing. It was like my ears hadn't woken up yet. Neither had my limbs. I couldn't feel any of them. Out of curiosity, I wiggled my toe. It took a while to form the thought then send the message from my brain to my toe. After a delay, my big toe wiggled against starchy fabric that felt nothing like my sheets at home.

My focus pulled to my breathing. Even that was a challenge. The rise and fall of my chest was slow and shallow. I couldn't have been getting enough air. I had to get up and start my day. A stretch and a scalding shower were in order. I usually skipped breakfast, but today I felt like I needed some.

There was a cart not far from the office. The little old man that ran it made the most delicious wraps stuffed with eggs, meat, and peppers. He'd even learned a few alien recipes. Maybe I'd grab something for Sk'lar on the way there.

There was a faint whirring sound. My ears finally caught up to the rest of me. I shut out every other thought to analyze the new sound.

Definitely mechanical. Designed to be quiet. I didn't feel a breeze or an unusual amount of warmth, so it wasn't a fan or a heater.

My eyes.

I'd forgotten I had eyes. They were closed. I needed to lift the lids. I could do that. It was simple.

Lifting my eyelids felt like lifting a rusted manhole cover with just two fingers. My vision was blurry at first. I blinked. Each blink felt like sandpaper over my corneas. When I winced, my whole face hurt.

"There she is," a deep, kind voice spoke. It sounded like there were three hundred gallons of water between me and whoever was speaking. I had to get through it. That voice, the speaker… that was someone important.

The words themselves reached my brain slowly. I looked in the direction that the voice came from.

Someone stood over my bed. Their skin was like coal but shot through with blue lines.

Sk'lar!

I blinked rapidly, ignoring the pain.

"Sk'lar," I croaked. Speaking felt as if the skin inside my throat was being torn open.

"Don't talk yet," Sk'lar advised. "Wait until you have some water. I'll go ask Evie if I can give you some."

He disappeared and reappeared a few minutes later with a white paper cup and a bendy straw. He held the cup steady while I tried to suck through the straw. It took me a few tries.

"What happened to me?" I asked once my throat felt better.

"You got shot."

"I. What?" My brows pulled together.

"At the last speech," Sk'lar explained. "Someone fired shots into the crowd. You and Vidia were both struck."

"Is she okay?" I tried to sit up, despite every bone and muscle in my body protesting.

Sk'lar placed a firm, but gentle, hand on my shoulder and pushed me back down into the pillows.

"She's okay," he assured me. "She's up and walking around already."

"Is that a roundabout way of telling me I got the worst of it?"

"Yes."

"What exactly happened to me?"

"Like I said, you got shot."

"Where did I get shot? Sk'lar, why won't you give me a straight answer?" I demanded.

"Because I don't want to cause you distress."

"Not telling me is what's causing distress," I insisted.

"Okay, okay." Sk'lar put his hands up in surrender, his eyes tight with worry. "The bullet missed your spine by an inch. Unfortunately, it was some kind of homemade round designed to split in half. One half nicked your heart. The other punctured your lung."

I took in a shuddering breath.

"You lost a lot of blood and you were in surgery for almost twenty-four hours. Evie brought in every medical expert on the planet to help save your life."

"I don't know what to say." I needed to say something. I'd freak out if I didn't. A bullet nicked my heart? It tore through my lung? I shouldn't be alive.

"You don't have to say anything." Sk'lar pushed back a lock of my hair. The sweetness of the gesture, the intimacy of it, stirred something in me.

Before everything went to hell, I'd been trying to figure out where he and I stood in a relationship. I thought I was fine with a friends-with-benefits arrangement to keep stress levels low after work. At least, I thought I was fine, until I realized we never explicitly agreed to a no-strings thing. Now I wasn't sure.

Did he want more than that?

Did I?

Did I just not understand my own feelings or was I under the influence of medical drugs? Why was this so hard to sort out?

"You all right?" Sk'lar asked, his voice comforting, even through the morass of my feelings.

"What?" I'd almost forgotten he was sitting right there.

"You're frowning at the wall. I'm worried you're going to give yourself a headache."

"Too late." I forced my face to relax and drink more water.

"Are you going to tell me what's on your mind?" he pressed.

"Nope."

"Do you want me to tell you about the man who shot you?"

"Yup."

Sk'lar laughed and scooted his stool even closer to my bedside.

"Is he dead?" I asked.

"No." He frowned. "Despite my opinions on the mater."

"He almost killed me. Why isn't he dead?" I demanded.

"Because he was taken in for questioning. And no matter how I felt, that was the reasonable, logical response."

My anger deflated. "Oh."

"His name is Canter Xent. He's one of the long-standing anti-alien radicals. He's been on our radar for a while, but we had no idea he was in the city."

"How is that possible?"

"That's what we want to find out," he explained. "Xent somehow bypassed all of our security and managed to get a clear shot at you and Vidia."

"Do you think he was hired by Dashiell Fox?" I asked.

"It's possible, but we can't confirm. He's not talking."

"Let me at him," I said through gritted teeth. "I'll get some words out of him."

"Words or screams of pain?"

"Does it matter?"

"Not to me, it doesn't. And it sure as skrell didn't matter to me as I was chasing him. If I'd gotten a hold of him…"

"You chased him?"

Sk'lar nodded.

"I didn't know you'd been hit at the time," he admitted. "If I had, I would've gone right to you. If I'd gotten to you right away, maybe the surgery time wouldn't have been so long."

"Don't worry about the surgery time." I reached out and touched his arm. "It's not like I was awake for it."

"Your heart stopped beating," Sk'lar blurted.

"What?"

"Twice, actually. Your heart stopped beating twice. I wasn't allowed in the room but I watched the whole thing through the security feed."

"You didn't have to do that." My throat grew tight.

"Yes, I did. If anything happened to you, I wanted to be there for you in whatever way I could." He took my hand in both of his and squeezed gently. I tried to squeeze back, but my grip was weak and my muscles weren't responding properly yet.

"Thank you." I didn't realize how much it meant to me that he was there until he said it. If I'd died on that operating table, I would've wanted someone close to me to be there.

We sat in silence together. I enjoyed silence, but it wasn't often I sat in silence so heavy with unsaid things.

Not sure what else to do, I cleared my throat.

"Do you need more water?"

"Please."

Sk'lar held the cup for me once more while I drank.

"What day is it?" I asked. "I was in surgery for nearly a day. How long ago was that?"

"A few days," he answered. "Evie kept you unconscious for the first forty-eight hours to speed recovery. We didn't expect you to wake up so quickly."

"But you were already in my room," I recalled. "If you weren't expecting me to wake up, why were you here?"

"Just to keep you company. I've been reading the news to you."

"I'm sorry to say that I didn't catch any of it," I teased. "What's the latest news?"

"Nothing exciting since the debate. Reporters are trying to get information about Canter Xent to print," he said. "General Rouhr won't give them anything."

"Good. I don't want an anti-alien radical gaining fame off this," I scoffed. "No other news?"

"It's election day, so there will be news in a little while."

"It's election day?" Once again, I tried to shoot up in bed, but Sk'lar stopped me and eased me back down.

"I wasn't going to tell you. I didn't want you to exert yourself," he sighed.

"You weren't going to tell me?" I snapped.

"Let me cycle back to not wanting you to exert yourself."

"If I stay calm, can I watch the election?" I bartered.

"Only if you promise not to move. Or yell. Or throw things."

"Do you think we're going to get bad news?"

"It's difficult to say," he said after struggling to find the right words.

"Why?"

"Since the shooting, nearly one-third of Ankau's citizens have come out as openly anti-aliens. Who knows how many are still keeping under wraps?"

I closed my eyes and tried to keep my breathing steady.

"There's no use getting agitated until the election happens." Sk'lar gave my hand another squeeze.

Until it was time to reveal the winner of the election, Sk'lar did his best to keep me distracted. He read reports from every corner of the planet, asked for advice on settlement security measures, and brought me more food than I could eat from the cafeteria.

When the election results were due to be announced, I couldn't breathe. If Vidia lost, everything we'd worked for would be for nothing. Dashiell Fox in charge would be a giant foothold for the anti-alien radicals.

A milky faced young woman sat in an official looking office with a datapad that automatically counted all the votes.

With a smile that was too large for her face, she looked at the broadcasting camera.

"The new Mayor of Nyheim is Vidia Birch!" she declared with enthusiasm I suspected was genuine.

I finally felt like I could breathe again.

"At least that's one thing we don't have to worry about," I said.

My energy seeped from my body in a wave. Sk'lar still held my hand. I ran my thumb across his palm and let my eyelids fall closed.

"Don't let me fall asleep, all right?" I mumbled. There was so much to plan. Vidia would be a bigger target now.

"Whatever you say," Sk'lar whispered, fingers laced through mine.

Within moments I was asleep.

SK'LAR

Twelve days had passed before Phryne, thanks to some Urai tech and her own resilience, was released from the hospital. She wasn't allowed to go back to work, at least not to do anything terribly stressful. She was cleared for light duty, essentially clerical-type stuff, and we all knew she wouldn't hold to that.

Even if I tried locking her in my apartment, which I'd seriously considered.

Vidia had come to me the day before. "What are you planning on doing for her when she's released tomorrow?"

"Well, since she's not allowed to return to full duty, and she won't be happy sitting at a desk for long, I figured I'd try to take her out to do something fun. But simple," I added quickly as Vidia started to glare.

Her mood lightened quickly. "Good. I don't want to see her here, at least not today. I want you to make sure that she relaxes. She's been trying to work from her hospital bed and, while I love her, I really do, I love her to death, she's getting to be a bit annoying and bossy. I know she's not going to be happy with not being around right now, especially since I've won the election and she'll want to figure out the security issues and whatnot, but she needs a day of nothing. Got that?"

With a smile and a repressed chuckle, I nodded. "I understand."

"Good," she said as she grabbed my arm and held it as she walked me around the office, her office, and out into the hallway. "I've arranged a shuttle for the two of you. There's a secluded beach, almost due north of here, you can't get to it without a shuttle, or climbing a few hundred feet down a sheer cliff-face. Take her there. Get her to relax and enjoy herself."

"Are you sure?"

She looked up at me as though I was a fool, and based on the look she gave me, I felt like a fool. "Really?" she asked.

I held up my hand. "Sorry. You know she's going to ask about who's watching over you. What should I tell her?"

"Tell her that Rouhr and Vrehx have it covered for now, and that while I know she'll always do a better job than they will, she needs to be at full-health before she comes back. Do that for me?"

I nodded. That had been yesterday. This morning, I waited for Phryne to exit the hospital.

"You are terrible at your job, you know that?"

I turned to my left, a smile plastered on my face as I watched Phryne walk gingerly towards me. "And how did you get out before you were supposed to?"

"Oh, please," she said as she hugged me. I returned her hug gingerly, remembering the bullet wound in her lower back. "The only reason I didn't leave a few days ago was because of Vidia. She basically told me that she'd replace me if I left before the doctors released me. I know she was lying, but still."

"You didn't want to risk her following through, especially now that she's mayor and has a political reputation to uphold?" I finished for her.

She nodded. "Yeah, something like that. So, not to change the subject, but what are you doing here?"

"Oh, you know, I came to visit some of the nurses, see if they could give me a sponge bath. Always wondered what that would feel like," I said with a smile.

"Ah, I see," she said with a wave of her hand. Then she looked up at me. "Better not be that little nineteen-year-old though, she's way too eager to please and she strikes me as the stalker, possessive type."

"Noted," I said with a nod. "Maybe I'll switch my attention to one of the patients instead. You wouldn't happen to know of one? Maybe recently released? Recovering from a gunshot wound or something of the sort?"

"Oh," she smiled at me. "You have a type? You like the injured ones, huh?"

I laughed. "Well, I figured if I was broken, I might go for someone slightly broken, as well."

She slapped me playfully. "You're not broken, jackass. Don't be an idiot."

I smiled as I picked up the bag I'd packed for her. "Come on, I have a surprise for you."

"Wait, what? I need to get to work," she protested as she followed me.

I shook my head. "No, you don't. Vidia has ordered you to take the day off and relax. She wants you to know that Rouhr and Vrehx are taking care of her security, for now, and that you should take a day to enjoy yourself before you get back to sitting your ass in a chair."

"She did not say that," Phryne said.

"Well," I shrugged. "I'm sort of paraphrasing. But she did still say that you need the day off, so I'm here to give you the day off."

"I don't need one," she protested as I kept walking with her stuff to where I had parked the car I'd borrowed. I got to the car, put her bag in the back, and opened the passenger door for her. She tried to protest, but I shook my head at her as she opened her mouth to talk. "You're not going to let me get out of this, are you?"

"Not a chance," I smiled. She got in, carefully, and I closed the door, then rounded the front of the car and got in.

"Where are you taking me then?"

"You'll see," I smiled again.

"You know, I hate that smile," she said. "It always means you're trying to be tricky."

I shrugged. "At least when I try to be tricky, it's done in an innocent way."

"Bullshit."

I laughed as I drove. I took her to the outskirts of town where we had set up a firing range. She looked at me, a mixture of pleasure and confusion in her eyes. "What's this?" she asked coyly.

"Just a place to have some fun," I answered. "And maybe to blow off some steam." She smiled that wonderful smile.

As I signed her into the firing range, she looked at the different weapons we had to choose from.

"Stay away from the big ones, don't want you back

in the hospital because you popped your stitches or something," I chuckled at her.

She stuck her tongue out at me, then picked out five different handguns and a rifle. "Think I can handle these?" she asked me teasingly.

I shrugged. "I guess we'll see."

Over the next three hours, we fired off a great many rounds and tried nearly every gun she was able to fire without hurting herself. I even showed her a few of the slightly bigger weapons we had that weren't personal weapons to any of the team members. I didn't think that, during any of the time that I'd known her, I had ever seen her smile so much. As she finished off her clips from the Heretic revolver she had chosen, I called in the shuttle that Vidia had set up for us. It landed as Phryne finished off her last rounds.

We cleaned up our stuff, handed off the weapons to the range master, then I took her to the shuttle.

"What's this?" she asked as we approached.

"The rest of your day off," I smiled. We boarded and I handed the keys to the car over to the shuttle pilot, Dax. He smiled and winked at me as we passed.

I lifted the shuttle up into the air, punched in the coordinates of the beach, then pushed the shuttle forward.

"Are you gonna tell me where we're going or not?" Phryne asked as we flew. I looked over at her as she leaned back in the seat, carefully resting her feet up onto the console, making sure not to touch anything.

"Well, since I get to look at you stretched out like that, maybe I'll hold off for a minute or two longer," I smiled.

"Ha. Tell me. Now."

I raised my eyebrows. "Hmm. Well, I guess. Since you asked so nicely," I smirked. "Vidia wanted me to get you to relax."

"You already said that."

"I did," I conceded. "Part of that relaxation is in that bag behind your seat."

She jumped and looked behind her. "Shit. I didn't even see the thing. What's in here?" she asked as she reached for it, wincing a bit as she turned her body too much.

"You okay?" I asked.

"Mm-hmm," she hummed. "Turned too much, that's all. So," she started, then pulled a bikini out of the bag. "I'm going to guess it has something to do with sun, water, and maybe a beach of some sort?"

"Aww, how did you guess?" I said in mock sadness.

"I don't know. Maybe I'm psychic or something?"

I laughed. She could do that, and I found myself enjoying that. After nearly an hour of flight, we landed at the beach. I left the shuttle to give her a chance to change, and when she came out, my jaw hit the ground.

She stood on the platform of the shuttle in a magnificent red and yellow bikini. She struck a pose that emphasized the muscles in her legs, the lean cut of the muscles in her torso, and the seamless tan of her skin.

"Like what you see?" she asked coyly.

I had no words, merely a dumbfounded nod. She walked up to me, placed a finger on my jaw, and closed my mouth for me.

"Well, are you going to join me?" she asked as she reached up and kissed me. "We're here, so we might as well enjoy the time and the privacy." She smiled as she smacked me on the butt and pushed me towards the shuttle.

I rushed over, changed into my shorts that were in the bag, and jogged back to the beach, where she was sitting just on the edge of the water. It was a gorgeous sight to behold.

PHRYNE

"One more set," Evie urged.

"I hate this," I growled.

"I know. That's why I'm making you do it."

I'd been in physical therapy with Evie for twelve days now. We started slowly with simple hand and foot movements from the confines of my hospital bed. I regained my strength more quickly than Evie had expected. At first, she was hesitant to move me to standing exercises so soon. Now she was more than happy to push me to my breaking point.

I took one step forward, planted my feet shoulder-width apart, stretched my right arm to my left foot, then did the opposite. The muscles around where the shot had pierced my back stretched and tightened in protest. I repeated the motion twenty times.

"I feel weak."

"Like your body can't take this?" Evie prompted.

"No, like I'm useless."

"You're far from useless," Evie assured me. "You sustained massive internal and muscle injuries. The only way you'll become useless is if you don't take the proper steps to heal. It's a balancing act. Push yourself too hard and you'll reinjure yourself. Push yourself too little and you won't regain your former strength."

"No amount of physical fitness will prevent me from trusting the wrong people."

"What do you mean?"

"I have to interview potential candidates for my alpha team when we're done here."

"That sounds exciting." I could tell from the smile on Evie's face that she didn't understand my meaning.

"Yeah," I said weakly. "Exciting."

I carefully selected the members of my team. Those chosen had my utmost trust and confidence. Two of them had betrayed me. Malkin had tried to murder Vidia and I felt certain he was involved in planning the siege on our building. I found out from Tona that Eirellya, Mekinna's cousin and another crucial member of my team, left the same day I was injured. Apparently, Dashiell Fox made sense to her.

Mekinna was devastated. Eirellya jumping ship put a strain on her close-knit family.

Cyrus was still with me, loyal as ever.

But for how long?

I pushed the thought away. If I started being suspicious of my team without evidence of their disloyalty, we'd unravel.

I had Ryx, as well. Ex-mercenary. Mean looking man, but as gentle as a lamb with his five-year-old twin girls. He already gave the alpha team more than I could ever ask of him. It wasn't fair of me to keep asking. I needed to find at least two more people to place on the alpha team.

"Maybe Sk'lar could help," Evie suggested.

I straightened up and gave her a quizzical look.

"How?"

"Well, you and he spend a lot of time together. He probably knows what sort of person you need and can give objective advice."

"We haven't spent that much time together." I shrugged off her words. I wasn't ready for other people to weigh in on the maybe-relationship between me and Sk'lar.

"He spent every day in the hospital," Evie smirked.

"True, but I was unconscious," I pointed out. "That's not what I'd call spending time together."

"Don't involve Sk'lar in the interviews, then," Evie laughed. "I'm not trying to force you into anything. I just want whatever will put the least amount of strain on you."

"Interviews aren't physically demanding."

"I meant emotional strain," Evie sighed.

"Right. Am I done?"

"Walk around the room a few times to cool your muscles out. After that, you're free to go."

After one lap around the room in awkward silence, I turned to Evie.

"Thanks for the advice. I know your intentions are good."

"You'll find that most people's intentions are good." Evie smiled knowingly.

"One can't be so sure anymore. The election changed a lot of things."

"I know. But we'll be okay. We survived the Xathi invasion, we survived the Puppet Master. We'll survive the ignorance of the masses."

"In many cases, ignorance kills more people than the blasters we carry."

"I haven't given you doctor's permission to carry the weight of the world on your shoulders," Evie smirked. "Focus on one thing at a time right now. Get through your interviews."

"Right. One thing at a time," I repeated.

Evie and I set our appointment for the following day and I proceeded back to my office. There was a line of potential alpha team candidates waiting at my door. With a reluctant sigh, I ushered the first of many into my office.

Vidia would tell me I wasn't giving any of the candidates a fair shot. None of them impressed me. Their qualifications were standard at best. Every time a new face appeared before me, all I could think about was the potential danger they brought with them.

The doe-eyed surveillance tech expert could've easily been an assassin hired by Dashiell Fox or any number of the anti-alien radicals. The tactile weapons expert that also happened to be built like a brick shithouse could've been a spy ready to betray all our classified information.

I flew through the candidates in record time, which wasn't good. When they were all gone, I walked down to Vidia's office. Evie was right. I wanted to talk to Sk'lar about everything, but he and the rest of his strike team were out working with Fen. The rifts were still acting up. I didn't know enough about how the rifts worked to be of assistance. Besides, General Rouhr and I agreed that at least one of us should be near Vidia at all times.

"How'd the interviews go?" she asked when I dragged myself into her office and threw myself melodramatically onto the spare chair. "That bad, huh?"

"I can't get out of my head enough to see each

candidate objectively," I confessed. "Everyone I don't know is now officially a threat."

"That way of thinking is what birthed the radicals," Vidia warned.

"We both got shot. I'm allowed to be hesitant."

"I know, I know." Vidia lifted her hands. "But tell me you at least kept their resumes."

"I kept their resumes."

"Good. Don't think about them anymore today. Go home. Go to bed."

"I could say the same to you."

"I'm the mayor, I don't get to go to bed."

I sat with Vidia for a short while longer, letting her chat about meaningless things. It made her feel better.

Night had fallen by the time I walked back to my apartment. With every step, I looked over my shoulder, expecting another attack. The person who'd tried to stab me was never apprehended. I wondered if it was Canter Xent.

Once home, I took a lukewarm shower. It was better for my muscles than my usual scalding hot shower.

I climbed into bed and stared up at my ceiling. I should've called Sk'lar. More often than not, he'd been spending nights at my place. We didn't go drinking beforehand anymore. Evie said no drinking while I was still in recovery. I slept better when Sk'lar was here. I liked feeling that there was someone near me to watch my back.

Sleep came slowly. When it did, it was far from sound.

I dreamed that something was in my bedroom. It had long black tendrils of energy that slid over my skin and left behind a tar-like substance. My skin itched and burned under its touch. At the center of the knot of tendrils was a dark shape with no distinct features. I would've guessed it was six feet tall. Maybe taller. I didn't know. It kept shifting in the darkness, winking in and out of existence.

When it touched my forehead, terrible thoughts appeared in my mind.

It showed me an image of myself standing over Vidia's dead body. It felt good. Right, even.

I saw flashes of the aliens tied up and gagged. General Rouhr was covered in bloody sores. Sk'lar was missing an eye.

Yes, this was right. This was how it was supposed to be.

I then saw images of our world rebuilt at last. Beautiful buildings towered up to the skies. The forests flourished once more. The Puppet Master was gone, the walking trees and other deadly creatures of the forest gone with it. We humans were the masters of the land. We'd built a utopia.

I was there. I had a whole team of perfect soldiers following my every word. No one was attacked in the streets. No one was shot by snipers. Everything was finally back to how it was supposed to be.

Yet, I felt empty. The images in my head should've been fulfilling, but they weren't.

Vidia and I were supposed to help people together. General Rouhr was supposed to be there, too.

In fact, the beautiful future I saw in my mind's eye wouldn't be possible without General Rouhr and his men. The humans needed the aliens. We needed their technology. We needed their knowledge of the universe.

I needed Sk'lar with me. I still didn't understand how I needed him, but I did need him.

I didn't want that picturesque future if the aliens weren't there to share it with us.

The images in my head flickered away and were replaced with images of cities burning. General Rouhr stood on a pile of human corpses, laughing. Vidia was bound and chained to his belt. Sk'lar and the other strike team members herded humans like cattle, whipping them just for the fun of it.

It was utterly ridiculous. General Rouhr would never do something like that. Neither would any of the aliens. With a surge of willpower, I shoved the images from my mind.

I sat up in bed. The motion was too sudden for my tender back muscles. With a wince, I fell back down against my pillows, one hand blindly groping for the light on my bedside table. I half expected to see the shadowy being I'd seen in my dreams standing at the foot of my bed.

I was alone in my room.

Even so, something in the air didn't feel right.

SK'LAR

As the bright light of the sun peeked through my windows and threatened to pierce my brain through my eyelids, I rolled over to my side and tried to rediscover the darkness that came with sleep. I couldn't find it.

I rolled myself out of bed and made my way through my morning routine. After relieving myself, I took my shower, brushed my teeth, got dressed, then made myself some breakfast. I looked at my calendar to see that it was what the humans called October thirteenth, which happened to fall on a Friday.

Some of the humans around here treated the day as if it was something special, which made no sense to me. It wasn't a holiday, and it wasn't anything special based, on what people told me. It was simply a day that dealt with superstitions.

Now, superstitions are something that all soldiers know something about. I had my own superstitions about going into battle, so the idea that Friday the Thirteenth was either a good luck day or a bad luck day for people was believable, but why they made such a big deal out of it was beyond me.

After I ate, I made my way to the general's office for one of our weekly meetings, sometimes even more often, or whenever the general decided that he needed to talk to us and work things through. Today would mark the third day this week that I would sit and meet with him.

As I walked through the part of the city where most of the *Vengeance* crew lived, I marveled at the amount of work being done to repair what the Puppet Master's vines had caused. This particular neighborhood looked untouched by the vines, as did two of the neighborhoods nearby. However, I was about to walk through a small neighborhood that was still working on fixing things, and the construction was loud.

As I passed through the construction area, I waved at several of the people that were working and they waved back at me. It felt good to have them wave back with smiles on their faces, it meant that they hadn't suddenly changed their minds about us. The number of people that had suddenly flipped their approval of us had grown recently, and it had started to include not just people that were friendly with us, but even some of the doctors and scientists that we had worked with, some of the security personnel that had helped to protect us and the city, and even some of the children that were always friendly with us had shifted their feelings quickly.

As I entered the offices, I looked at Tobias with a bit of trepidation, but when he responded with his usual smile and happy demeanor, I relaxed and smiled back at him. I proceeded to the general's office, knocked, and walked in.

"Good morning, Sk'lar," Rouhr said as I entered.

"Morning, sir," I returned. He directed me to the couch as he rose from his desk and headed over. As I sat on the couch, he sat in his chair and pressed a button on his intercom. He quickly ordered breakfast, looking at me to silently ask if I wanted anything. I shook my head and he finished his order. I had noticed that he'd taken to eating breakfast here more often than not, and I sometimes wondered if he was even sleeping here more than he was at the home he shared with Vidia.

"First of all, how's Phryne doing?"

I let out a sigh. "She's not happy. With constantly having to change out her team because people are suddenly changing, it's making her apprehensive and nervous about things."

"I can imagine," he said as he took a drink from the cup of coffee at his side. "I wish I could offer her some of our own people, but we're spread thin already. I've got as many people as I can spare trying to keep an eye on Vidia already."

I nodded. As I was about to say something, the door opened and in walked Tobias with Rouhr's breakfast order. "Morning, sir."

"Tobias? What are you doing getting my breakfast?"

"I had a message to deliver anyway, so I figured I'd bring the food to you," Tobias answered as he set down the tray.

"Okay. What do you have?"

"Well, sir," Tobias started as he removed the tray lid. "Zarik wanted to report that there has been a break-in at one of the food kitchens. Nothing was taken, but the inside of the kitchen was vandalized with anti-alien sentiment and two of the range-tops were broken."

"Skrell. Anything on the surveillance?"

Tobias nodded sadly. "Unfortunately, sir, it was one of the employees. Within minutes of locking up and leaving, they broke in and vandalized the kitchen."

"Rek," I said, then immediately held up a hand in apology. "My apologies, sir."

Rouhr shook his head. "No apologies needed. That

was my identical reaction." He turned to Tobias. "Thank you, Tobias. Let Zarik know that, if possible, I want him to try to find help for fixing the kitchen."

"Yes, sir," Tobias said as he headed out of the door.

Rouhr turned back to me. "Rek. This is getting ridiculous."

"I agree. What are the other team leaders saying?"

"Nothing," he responded. "They have the same information that we do, and so far, the same ideas that we have. We're all at a loss here. What if Fen was right? Was the use of the rifts the cause?"

"I don't know, sir."

"If it was," he continued on, almost as if I hadn't said anything, "then I'm responsible because I'm the one that called for the rifts."

"You are not responsible," I said forcefully to get him to look at me. "Sir, there could be no way that you knew that the rifts would do this, if they indeed *have* done this. And, you weren't the only one to call for the rifts. All three of us, as team leaders, we called for the rifts several times ourselves. Not to mention that Fen was the one in charge of the rift device and she was the one that opened each and every rift we called for."

"I know that, I do," Rouhr said over a bite of eggs. "But if the rift is responsible, as General, I could have put a restriction on the number of times we used it and that could have helped to prevent this situation from getting as bad as it's gotten."

"Sir, don't put all the blame on yourself. There could be another reason for all of this," I said.

"What?"

"What if we didn't stop the synthetic brain-wipe stuff they were using?" I suggested. "What if someone else continued to make it and found a way to make it work faster? That could be a possibility, could it not?"

He sat there and visibly thought about it for a few moments. "That could be a possibility, yes." The more he thought about it, the more he nodded in agreement. "That just might absolutely be what is happening here."

"So, we just need to find out if there is someone creating more of that synthetic stuff and using it on people," I said.

Rouhr's face lit up for a moment, then fell. "Wait. If they're using the synthetic mind-wipe stuff, then what about what happened with Phryne last night?"

"What happened to her last night?"

"Apparently she had a bad dream of something trying to invade her mind," Rouhr told me. "She told Vidia about it an hour ago. Vidia told me. The thing is, if someone gave her some sort of synthetic juice, they either gave it to her through some food she had, something she drank, or snuck into her place and gave it to her that way."

An ice-cold chill ran up my spine. The idea that someone possibly targeted Phryne specifically, that scared me. "So, where do we look?"

"What about that compound you said you saw? The one where the ship used to be," Rouhr said.

It took me a second to remember. "I remember it. You want to start looking there?" Currently, it was the only place we knew of for sure that was anti-alien that was close by. All of the other anti-alien establishments had moved and established themselves far away. Unless they were shuttling in, that compound was the closest place.

"I do," Rouhr said. "We might be able to find something there that could answer our questions."

"Might be worth looking into," I said.

"Good. I want you and your team suited up and ready to go in thirty," he said as he stood up and made his way back to his desk. "Make sure the pilot is not human, don't want them switching on us mid-flight."

"Understood, sir," I said as I stood up. Then, "Wait, 'us', sir?"

"That's right," Rouhr responded. "I'm going with you."

"Are you sure that's prudent, sir?" I asked. "As much as it pleased me to go into battle with you recently, with everything going on, you would want to come with us?"

"Are you seriously trying to say that I can't go with

you?" The general hit me with a stare, and while I wasn't normally one to back down, I knew better than to challenge my commander.

Even if I wasn't entirely happy about his decision.

"Not at all, sir," I answered. "I am more than willing to take you wherever you wish to go, sir."

He chuckled. "Good answer. I think it's important that I go with you till this threat is neutralized. Thirty minutes, clear?"

"Clear, sir."

PHRYNE

"I need your help." Vidia stood in my office doorway with a pleading look.

"What is it?" I was out of my seat in an instant, my hand already reaching for the weapon at my hip.

"Nothing dangerous!" Vidia quickly clarified.

"Oh." I relaxed my stance. "Then what is it?"

"There's a tiny problem in some of my reports. I was hoping you'd be able to help me sort it out."

"Of course."

I followed Vidia to her office. There were datapads strewn all over her desk. I picked up the one nearest to me and gave it a look over.

"This doesn't look like a report." I frowned. "This looks like a budget."

"It is." Vidia plopped back into her chair. I took the spare.

"Where are the reports?"

"These *are* the reports. The budget reports."

"Budgeting isn't in my job description," I laughed. "It's not an area of expertise, either."

"I know, but you can read and do basic math, therefore you can help me." Vidia eyed me over the top of a datapad.

"I still don't understand."

"With the surge of anti-alien support, much of my funding has suddenly disappeared."

"I see."

"And the security budget has been through the roof for months on end."

"Don't blame me for that," I snorted. "I submit all of my anticipated costs for approval before I arrange anything."

"We have to do some serious rearranging," Vidia tutted.

"Are you sure there's no one more qualified than me to help you with this?"

"I'm the most qualified person for this," she laughed. "I don't need your expertise. I need your hands."

"My hands?"

"For data input."

"I'm a very busy person, you know?"

"I know. If you'd rather spend all day finding new members for your alpha team, I'll happily let you go."

I dreaded the thought of another round of interviews. Sk'lar had recommended a few members from the city patrol team to stand in on my alpha team until I found the perfect replacements.

"I can spare a few minutes."

"That's what I thought."

For the next three hours, I plugged numbers into various applications at Vidia's direction.

"The last thing I want is to decrease the budget for the housing construction," Vidia said.

"We can always cut the food," I suggested.

"Have you seen the way those aliens eat?" she snorted. "They'd riot."

"What about the produce? We can start growing our own with those planters. I bet Leena could whip up something to accelerate growth and output."

"That would mean revoking income from the produce suppliers we already use. We're their biggest customers."

"I told you I'm no good at this."

"You're doing great. Keep proposing alternatives for me to shoot down."

"That doesn't sound as fun as you think it does."

"Maybe not to you."

Over the course of the next two hours, I looked through the budgets for places to cut funding while Vidia looked for ways to generate revenue. The problem was that there weren't many citizens able to give anything. All of Vidia's projects were designed to provide relief, not generate profit.

"We simply can't cut anything," Vidia groaned. "Not without detrimental side effects."

"Fen and her people are self-sustaining. Maybe she'd be willing to share some tips or loan some tech to help us cut costs."

"There's a big difference between sustaining a dozen individuals and sustaining a large city."

"You don't need to sustain the city yet. You have to sustain this building and our operations."

"But eventually, I'll have to sustain the city. I have a few more tricks to try before I throw in the towel and sell all of my belongings to fund us. Until then, can we talk about something else? My head's going to explode."

"Are you sure distracting conversation is the best thing right now?"

"I wasn't being figurative when I said my head is going to explode," Vidia repeated.

"Okay, okay. We'll talk about something else." I shook my head and laughed.

"You're bad at talking," Vidia declared after five minutes of silence.

"You already knew that about me."

"I know something we can talk about." Vidia lifted her gaze from the three datapads she held at once and flashed a conspiratorial smile.

"Why are you looking at me like that?"

"I want to talk about Sk'lar."

"What about him?" I looked back at my datapad, blushing.

"I want to know what's going on between the two of you to make you blush like that."

"Nothing's going on between us."

"Right. That's why he spent as much time as he possibly could at your bedside after your surgery. Totally reasonable."

"We're friends," I shrugged. "We've been working together a lot. It's only natural a friendship would develop."

"For everyone else on the planet, yes. But not you. For as long as I've known you, you've gone to great lengths to keep your personal and professional life separate."

"But you and I are friends. That disproves your statement."

"Remember how we became friends? I kept

approaching you to start conversations. I asked you to go out to lunch or to get coffee before work."

"I remember. You were extremely pushy."

"I needed to be. You wouldn't have become my friend otherwise."

"Why did you go to all that effort?"

"Because you were coming off a little sociopathic in the workspace," Vidia laughed. "You needed a friend and I needed a friend who was as intelligent and driven as I was. Match made in heaven. Stop steering the conversation away from Sk'lar."

"Damn it." She caught me. "If you really want to know, we occasionally engage in casual sex."

Vidia tipped her head back and laughed.

"So, you fuck?"

"I wouldn't say-"

"Screw."

"Well-"

"Hook up."

"Vidia!"

"What? You can't expect me not to tease you for what you just said."

"There's nothing wrong with what I said." I crossed my arms defensively. I knew I was being childish, but this sort of conversation was uncharted territory.

"You sound like you're filing an official report, not talking about your bang buddy."

"Fine! Yes, we fuck!" I exclaimed.

"Thank you. But that doesn't explain why he refused to leave your side when you were in the hospital."

"General Rouhr would've done the same if that was you in the bed instead of me."

"Yes, he would've," Vidia nodded. "But Rouhr and I aren't casually screwing. We're going to be together for the rest of our lives. See the difference?"

"Sk'lar and I aren't going to be together for the rest of our lives," I said quickly.

"Are you sure about that?" Vidia asked with a knowing smile.

"Yes! But hypothetically speaking, even if I wanted to be in a real relationship with him, I wouldn't know how to make that transition."

"Right, hypothetically speaking." Vidia fixed me with a piercing stare. I immediately started to squirm.

"Okay, okay! It's not hypothetical at all." I caved. "How do you do that?"

"I received enhanced abilities when I decided to become a politician."

"Very funny." I narrowed my eyes at her.

"Have you talked to Sk'lar about this?"

"Between the siege, the election, and getting shot, there hasn't been an abundance of time." I rolled my eyes.

"Yeah, I'm sure while you were quite busy confined to your hospital bed."

"I didn't know what to say," I admitted in defeat. "I don't even know if he wants something more than casual. Casual works for us."

"Are you sure casual works for him?" Vidia pressed. "Or is he just waiting for you to make a move?"

"I don't know." I placed my head in my hands. "Why does this have to be so complicated?"

"Because you're making it complicated. Rouhr and I are both busy people. We didn't have time to dance around each other playing silly games with our affections. When we both realized we had feelings for each other, we talked about it. We had to put some aspects of our relationship on hold, since the Xathi invasion was still in full swing, but we still talked."

"I'm not the best at talking," I mumbled.

"How are you when you usually talk to Sk'lar? You must not be as bad as you think if he's still hanging around."

"Usually we have a few drinks while we talk."

"Okay. Try it without the drinks next time. Talk openly. Don't build walls around yourself like you always do."

"What if he doesn't feel the same way?"

"That's always a possibility." Vidia reached across her desk to give my arm a squeeze. "But if you want my opinion, and I know you do because you're hopeless without my guidance."

"Hey!"

"Sk'lar truly cares about you. You need to give him a fair chance."

"You're right," I sighed. "He deserves that much."

"So you deserve that much, too."

SK'LAR

We were only in the air for a short time before we arrived at the crater where our home used to be.

The last time we'd been here, the rim of the crater had been taken over by an anti-alien faction.

Yet now, the compound was empty.

The shuttle landed and we all exited, weapons at the ready. Yet no one was here.

"Where is everyone?" Navat asked.

"This doesn't seem right," Tyehn added. "Something is wrong."

I had to agree with both of them. Something seemed wrong. The compound seemed to be abandoned, empty of anything living. "General, I believe it would be best if you were to stay here."

"Really? Don't try to treat me like an old man," Rouhr scoffed at me. "I'm not quite there, Sk'lar. Let's check this place out."

"Yes, sir," I said. I motioned for the rest of the team to spread out as I stayed close to the general. We moved through the compound quickly, clearing it in less than ten minutes.

"Nothing, sir. It's all clear," Jalok said to the general.

Rouhr looked at me and I shook my head. "I'm as lost as you are," I said to him. I looked at everyone else. "Was there anything?"

A collective shake of their heads, until Tyehn shrugged. "I might have found something."

"What?"

"In one of the makeshift sheds, I found a lot of digging equipment that looks like it's been used recently."

Rouhr took a step forward. "Show us."

As Tyehn and Cazak led the way, I motioned for Jalok and Navat to bring up the rear. "Stay alert," I told them as we got to the shed that Tyehn had found.

"Here we go sir," I heard Tyehn tell the general.

I looked back to see the shed. Inside were numerous shovels, drills, and a small, portable digger. "Any idea how much digging they could have done with this?" Rouhr asked as I looked at the equipment.

"Not sure," I answered. "It all depends on how long they had to dig."

"Well," Tyehn interrupted. "That's not the only factor to take into account. We need to also consider how many people were digging, what the consistency of the ground was wherever they were digging, *then* we count in how long. They could have been digging for the last two days if they had enough people digging in a spot soft enough."

"He has a point," Cazak added.

"Okay, okay," Rouhr said. "Do we have any idea where they might have been digging and what for?"

We all shook our heads.

"Then I suggest we spread out and look for their dig site," Rouhr said. "Keep comms open, but stay quiet so everyone can hear what's happening. Activate tracers, as well."

I hated using the tracers. It wasn't that they weren't a smart tactic and that they didn't have their uses. I hated them because they were connected to our comms and they always created a buzzing noise in my head. After a while, the buzzing became highly annoying and drove me crazy. I hated them.

I activated my comm and my tracer as we spread out. Six different directions to the edge of the trees, then we began our search pattern. "Clockwise pattern, people," Rouhr said quietly into his comm. I took a quick look to my left, then proceeded to move to my right, looking for anything that might show either a dig site or a heavily used trail that might lead to something.

I was maybe halfway to Tyehn's starting location when Rouhr came on over the comms. "I found it. Get here, quietly and quickly." He clicked off the comm and we made our way to Rouhr's location beacon. Navat was the last to arrive, as he had been the furthest away.

What we looked at was a massive dig site in the cover of the trees. There was a fifty-foot run leading down into a hole that went dark quickly. At least six different mounds of earth filled in some of the empty spaces between the trees.

"Looks like we found it," Navat said needlessly. I looked at him like he was an idiot, then shook my head.

"Lock and load. Navat, since you've got the big mouth, you can take point. I'll back you," I said. "Jalok and Cazak, you two bring up the rear."

"You're not thinking of leaving me behind just because I'm in charge, are you?" Rouhr asked, a little bit of venom in his voice.

"Of course not, sir," I said. "You're right behind me." I motioned for Navat to lead the way.

We entered the tunnel, moving carefully. Each of us had our rifles at the ready, except for Cazak, who preferred his handgun. We travelled what must have been nearly a mile into the earth before Rouhr tapped my shoulder. I tapped Navat's shoulder, stopping him.

"What's the matter, sir?" I whispered.

Rouhr shook his head. "I've been trying to contact Puppet Master while we're down here, to see if he has any information for us. I'm not making contact."

"Is that normal?"

He shook his head again. "No. Ever since our introduction, once the Puppet Master enters your mind and speaks to you, he can converse telepathically with you anywhere on the planet. I usually can initiate a conversation by reaching out to him and thinking thoughts. He can, in times of great urgency, send a message to someone who has never been exposed to him. But he always answers me within seconds. Except this time. Something's not right down here."

I nodded, then motioned for Navat to lead on. The tunnel was straight, very few turns, yet it consistently angled downwards. There were a few places where they tunneled straight down, a makeshift wooden ladder to help bring people either down or back up.

After nearly an hour of traversing the tunnel, albeit slowly, Navat held up his hand and got down into a crouch. "I think I hear something up ahead."

That was my cue. "I'll take a look," I said. I moved forward another fifteen yards and came to the only corner in the entire tunnel. I risked a glance around the corner and saw maybe two dozen humans in one of the caverns that the Puppet Master had created for us to speak with him. In front of the humans was a cluster of vines that seemed to be gyrating in an uncontrollable fashion. When a few of the humans moved, I saw what looked to be a portable generator on the ground emitting something from it.

I waved for the others to come forward and met them five yards from the corner. "There's maybe two dozen, and they have some sort of generator that's making a cluster of vines act abnormally."

"What do you mean 'abnormally'?" Rouhr asked.

"They're gyrating, sort of like we do when we're being hit by one of the tasers that Tona and Skit showed us," I answered.

Rouhr's eyes went wide. "They're attacking the Puppet Master. Move," he ordered without waiting for us. He was at the corner within a few steps, opening fire.

We had made a switch to non-lethal rounds in our weaponry when people began changing suddenly. We wanted to make sure that if we were forced to fight one of our friends, we didn't kill them.

However, they weren't sharing the same mentality. Their rounds were real, as the scratch from the bullet grazing my wrist could attest to. I quickly took aim, fired, and took some pleasure that when my target fell backwards, he took three others down with him with his flailing. Tyehn shot three more in quick succession, each one hit in the solar plexus. As those three lay on the ground gasping for air, Navat and Cazak rushed in, handguns blazing as non-lethal rounds found their targets.

Once the fight was over, some forty seconds after Rouhr rushed around the corner, every one of the humans were down. Tyehn, Navat, and Cazak were all binding the humans as I looked at Jalok, who had taken a round to his left arm. It wasn't bad, the bullet had barely penetrated his scales. A quick wrap was all that was needed. As I was tying the bandage, a gunshot rang out. All five of us had our weapons pointed at Rouhr before we realized what had happened.

He had destroyed the generator, and the vines behind us stopped gyrating. Within seconds, Puppet Master's voice filled our minds. *"I thank you, my friends."* However, before we could hear anything else from him, a massive humming sound began to emanate from the generator.

Rouhr looked at it in confusion for a split second, then yelled "Run!" As we started to run for our lives, I saw the vines cover the humans. We were maybe halfway down the line when the generator exploded. The shockwave from the blast shook the ground around us, knocking us off our feet.

"Cover!" I yelled out as I covered my own head. The tunnel collapsed on top of us, burying us in who knows how much dirt. My mind immediately broke into a panic as I tried to dig myself out. I was buried. I couldn't breathe. I couldn't move. The air was disappearing, my mind was shutting down, I couldn't think.

I couldn't even feel the vine that wrapped itself around my arm and pulled me out of the dirt. As I lay there, hyperventilating and struggling to get my mind back, I could hear some of the conversation that Rouhr was having with Puppet Master. There was something about the generator causing him tremendous pain, but there only being the one. Something else about having a few prisoners, but I couldn't piece it together.

My mind was racing, my heart was pounding, all I could think about was being covered in so much dirt. I looked at the others to see them looking similar to how I felt.

At least I wasn't the only one to have been stressed out by being buried alive.

PHRYNE

Several days had passed since I'd spoken to Vidia about how I truly felt for Sk'lar. When I'd walked out of Vidia's office that day, I didn't want to follow her advice. Sk'lar meant a lot to me, I wasn't going to deny that any longer. My feelings for him were true and deep. The last thing I wanted was to put my relationship with him in jeopardy. At first, I believed the best way to do that was to tell him nothing and let things carry on as they always had.

But then I didn't see him that day. Or the day after that. In fact, it had been almost a week since I'd last seen him. We spoke when we could, through comm units or messengers. It was fine, but I found myself missing his company. I missed seeing him smile when I said something witty. I missed beating him at pool. I missed sleeping next to him at night.

I hadn't had another dream like the one I had the other night, but that didn't make sleeping alone any easier. If I wasn't working such late nights every night, I'd invite him over, but for the last couple of nights, I'd been working past three in the morning. Sk'lar had to report in at sunrise in order to get to Fen and the *Aurora* crash site before too much of the day had passed.

When I approached my office that morning, I saw a fresh line of new applicants for my alpha team. Two days ago, I finally hired two replacements for the alpha members that had turned on me. Benta and Nast were supposed to start training yesterday, but Mekinna injured her knee.

She slipped on her wet kitchen floor at home. One of the most highly trained professionals on the planet slipped at home. Of all the damn things that could've happened. According to Evie, Mekinna shattered her kneecap, and she had to be on desk duty for the next three months.

I hadn't gotten a chance to tell Sk'lar about Mekinna's unfortunate turn of events. I was sure he'd think it hilarious, if only for the fact that it forced me to continue my interview process. At least, this time I wasn't looking for a permanent replacement. That didn't make sitting through interviews any easier.

Many of the applicants were wildly underqualified for the position. That wasn't completely their fault. I required extensive combat knowledge and weaponry knowledge, as well as a page-long list of characteristics that most people didn't possess. Vidia thought my list was too specific, but that list was what built the alpha team that kept her alive.

I sat across my desk from a perky girl who turned out to be one of the operations interns. As grating as her voice was, she was already familiar with the buildings and standard protocols. I felt safer bringing her onto the team.

"Report for training with Cyrus tomorrow morning. Be there before dawn."

"Are you serious?" Her eyes bulged out as her voice reached a pitch only a forest creature could hear. "I got the job?"

"You will be a temporary replacement for Agent Mekinna while she's recovering from her injury, that's all."

"I won't let you down!" She leaped up and opened her arms.

"No hugging."

"Sorry." She tucked her arms back to her sides. "Thank you so much for the opportunity."

"Don't be late for training," I said by way of dismissal.

She skittered out of the office. I hope I hadn't made a mistake.

I'd interviewed over forty applicants that day. Tired and burned out on all forms of socialization, I shuffled home. As always, I looked over my shoulder every other step. My heart pounded as I walked the short distance between work and home and didn't calm down until I was safely through my front door.

My living room was lit with half a dozen candles. In the center of the room stood Sk'lar, holding two glasses.

"What are you doing here?" I grinned

"What a nice way to greet me," he laughed.

"I'm sorry! You surprised me. You know how I get when I'm not in control of every little thing."

"Yes, I do. Hence the spirits." Sk'lar lifted the glasses in his hand and passed one to me. I took a sip of the rich red liquid.

"This is exactly what I needed after today."

"Bad day?"

"Mekinna shattered her kneecap and I had to find a temp," I explained.

"A whole extra day of interviews?"

I nodded and plopped down onto my couch.

"Poor thing." He sat down next to me. I threw my legs across his lap.

"What's that smell?"

"I'm cooking dinner."

"I never cook here," I pointed out.

"I know. All the appliances are in pristine condition. I'm sure the food stall has already prepared your usual nightly serving of fried fish and sweet veggies."

"They'll be so sad when I don't show up."

"They'll live."

"What are you making instead?"

Sk'lar puffed his chest out. Whatever he'd made, he was damn proud of it.

"I made grilled skyflier with bassa root noodles and yellow petal sauce."

"Wow. I haven't eaten that well in years. I can't wait to try it."

"You don't have to wait. It's ready now." I lifted my legs so Sk'lar could get up. He walked over to my oven and opened it to reveal a tray of food. A tray which didn't belong to me.

"Did you buy a pre-cooked meal?" I smirked.

"Believe me, it's better this way." He pulled the tray out of the oven and served up two plates.

We ate on the couch, talking about everything except work. For once, I was sick of thinking about my job.

I knew Vidia recommended talking to Sk'lar about our relationship without the help of alcohol, but Sk'lar had gone to all the trouble to bring spirits. When the bottle was empty, I twisted myself on the couch so that I could look him in the eyes. Our knees touched.

"I want to talk to you about something," I said.

"I want to talk to you about something, too."

"Let me go first. I'll chicken out if I don't go first."

"I don't think that'll be the case."

I didn't know what he meant by that but I was still determined to go first.

"Please?"

"Oh, all right." Sk'lar rolled his eyes and grinned. "I'm a slave to your whims, after all."

"I like you," I spoke before fully absorbing what he'd just said.

"I like you, too."

"No, I mean I *really* like you. I like you as in a fall-asleep-thinking-of-you way and in a think-about-you-when-I-wake-up way. I like you so much that I might actually love you."

I clamped my lips shut too late to stop the words.

"I-"

Sk'lar put a finger over my lips.

"I like you in a can't-fly-my-aerial-unit-straight-because-I'm-thinking-of-you way and in a dream-about-you-every-night way. I also like you so much I might actually love you, too."

He removed his finger from my lips and pulled my face to his. Our lips met gently at first but quickly deepened into something smoldering and eternal. As he kissed me, he removed one hand from my face and picked up our empty plates. He set them on my coffee table then lay back on my couch, pulling me with him.

I flattened my body against his. My arousal flared to life when I felt the hardness of him pressing between my legs. I moved my legs to either side of him and sat up straight. I rocked my hips against him as he lifted my shirt over my head.

With some effort, we removed the rest of our clothing.

"Wait," I said as he removed one of his boots. "Leave the other boot on."

Sk'lar laughed and lay back down on the couch.

I wasted no time lowering myself onto him. After everything that had happened to us together and separately, I wanted nothing more than to lose myself in the feeling of him inside me. Sk'lar gripped my hips and held me on top of him for a moment.

"I've missed this," he moaned.

Slowly, he lifted my hips so that he could thrust up into me. Once we found our rhythm, he moved one hand to gently stroke and tease my breasts. I tipped my head back, letting the pleasure take me.

I placed my hands flat on his chest, marveling over how his muscles stretched and contracted underneath me. The hand that was on my breasts moved around to my back. Careful to avoid the sore spot left by the bullet, he pulled me down against him. I kissed his neck, his chest, and up to his jaw. When our lips fused together again, Sk'lar grabbed my hips and sank himself deep inside me.

I arched against him, crying out in ecstasy. Within moments, I was teetering on the brink of my climax. As if he knew, Sk'lar slowed down enough to pull me away from my peak of pleasure. He drove me to the edge and pulled me back over and over until I begged him for release.

When it came, my body gave into him completely. It wasn't until I tightened around him and felt him reach his own peak that I allowed my muscles to go slack.

Sk'lar held me against his chest. He stroked my hair and traced his fingers softly over my bare back. My breathing came in hard puffs and my legs were like gelatin.

He gently lifted me off him and resituated me on my side with my back against his chest.

Within moments, I was asleep.

SK'LAR

The temporal implant sent a light dose of PER hormone through my system, awakening me at precisely one hour after dawn. Phryne's lithe, warm body pressed against my own as she continued to slumber in my arms.

Outside her bedroom window, the whole world was going crazy. But right here, in my own—in *our* own—private world, things couldn't be better.

Stroking her hair softly, I gazed down at Phryne's lovely face. This feeling, this intimacy, was something I never thought I would have. Getting close to other sapient beings had never been my strong suit.

Even among the members of my own team, there was a certain distance. Certainly, I'd trust any of them with my life; that's what soldiers do for each other. We took care of our own. But loyalty wasn't the same as love.

I had friends, but none whom I felt as close to as I did to Phryne. In fact, even among my closest companions, I'd always felt like an outsider.

But Phryne's strangeness seemed to mesh well with my own, like two pieces that don't fit the rest of the puzzle but snap right together with each other.

Perhaps I was only made the leader of Team Three because they needed a K'ver and no one else was dumb enough to want the job. That didn't matter anymore. What did matter was that I had found someone whom I could be comfortable with, and that was worth all of the plum assignments in the world.

My perfect match.

My mate.

The delicate curves of her body enticed me. Though I knew I should let this busy woman sleep, I couldn't help but kiss her softly on the shoulder. Her body stirred in my arms and her eyes fluttered open as my kisses moved up to her neck.

Phryne enveloped me in her embrace, kissing me on the lips. She was aggressive, seeking control, as she plied her tongue with aplomb into my mouth. The flavor of the wine we'd had the previous night was still on her breath. Her hands slid all over my chest as we continued to taste each other.

But then I surprised her. I took control, rolling her over onto her back and winding up on top. Her face split in a wonderful smile, eyes half-lidded as she looked up at me. I kissed her firmly on the mouth once more, then moved downward. Phryne gasped as my lips blazed a trail across the delicate skin of her neck. Gently suckling on her skin, I moved down further still.

Her tight, toned body felt so good against my own. I was already responding, my member growing hard as an iron spike. Though my body urged me to take her, invade her, I controlled my impulses. I wanted to make her feel good. Besides, I was sure to find relief soon enough.

My lips traveled over her small but firm breasts. I carefully kissed each of her nipples before latching on like a nursing infant. Phryne gasped, arching her back as I attended to her body. My hand slid across her curved spine, enjoying every bump and ripple.

At a snail's pace, I worked my way down from her breasts, over the hard knots of muscle in her abdomen. She giggled when my tongue tickled her belly, but she made no move to stop me. Down, down I went, until I buried my face into the musky haven of her pussy.

"Oh, fuck, you're so good at that." Phryne's voice was thick with lust. Her nether lips were glistening wet with moisture that was only partly my saliva, slightly parted and revealing the pink softness within.

Animalistic grunts escaped my throat as I tasted her sweet arousal. My lips suckled at her outer labia, stretching the pliant flesh. Phryne's nails dug into the back of my head, almost as if she wanted to press me as tightly into her body as she could.

I gladly obliged. My face was buried in her smoothly shaven area as my nostrils filled with her musky aroma. Some part of my mind wondered if all human females shaved their pubic hair as some sort of ritual. I wasn't sure how I'd bring that up in conversation.

Anyway, my lips were otherwise occupied. Using my tongue, I traced circles around the mound of her clitoral hood. The little pink bulge grew larger, swelling with the heat of desire.

"What are you waiting for?"

Phryne's voice held great urgency as her body writhed beneath me, but I was not done teasing her yet. Who knew when we would get another opportunity like this to explore one another? I blew gently across her clitoris and Phryne let out a frustrated groan.

"Lick my clit, Sk'lar."

"No."

She moaned, body tensing up as she fought to achieve climax.

"You have to say 'please.'"

"You're so mean." Phryne's voice was husky, her tone desperate. "Please."

"Please what?"

"Oh god. Please, lick my clit, Sk'lar."

"Good girl."

My purple tongue flicked over the engorged organ, and the whole mass quivered delicately. I traced spiral patterns over its slick surface, even as my fingers pried her pussy lips wide open. I wanted to know all of her body, every inch.

Phryne's breathing came faster, sweat glistening on both our bodies mingled as I intensified my ministrations. When I took her entire clit, hood and all, inside of my mouth and softly applied suction, she came hard, without warning.

Phryne's body shook like a leaf in the wind, and I continued to suckle her clit until she came two more times. I looked up between her thighs, beyond her wonderful breasts, into her satisfied face.

"Did you like that, my dearest?"

"Yes." Her eyes narrowed, growing crafty, and then she pushed me up into a sitting position. "Almost as much as you're going to enjoy this."

Phryne knelt, then bent her head and took the dark indigo tip of my cock inside of her mouth. She rolled her eyes up to meet mine, intently watching for my reaction. The sight of her so eagerly trying to please me with her mouth nearly made me come right away, but I managed to stave it off. I wanted to enjoy this for as long as I could hold out.

Phryne wrapped one of her hands around my veined, circuitry-traced shaft, while the other cradled my sack. Being supported and handled in such an intimate way was an amazing experience, and again the ecstasy of being with someone washed over me.

Phryne's head bobbed up and down on my cock, taking nearly half of its length into her mouth with each stroke. Little gurgles escaped from her mouth when the head of my cock hit the back of her throat, but she didn't seem too distressed. In fact, her enthusiasm for her task grew.

"I—I can't hold back any more."

In response, I expected her to quickly disengage so as to avoid a mouthful of my seed. Instead, she took almost my entire cock into her mouth until it packed her throat. Then she came back off me slowly, her tongue playing with the underside, and my body released its pent-up energy. I came in her mouth, and she swallowed the entirety of the load.

Phryne pulled my cock out of her mouth and shot me a grin full of self-satisfaction. It was as if she was saying 'see, I can make your body do things, too'. Normally, I needed time to recover after an ejaculatory response, but her hands were working hard, pumping my shaft and getting me hard all over again.

"I hope you didn't think you were going back to sleep just because I gave you a blow job."

"A curious—ah—a curious human phrase, because you did more of a suction than an expulsion."

"Shut up, nerd."

My rod was hard as a rock once more, and she released my shaft. Phryne turned about in a half circle, presenting her shapely bottom to me. She put her head on the mattress and lifted her tail to the heavens.

"Come on, Sk'lar—violate me."

I slapped my hand on the side of her smooth ass and guided the head of my shaft between her eager, dripping wet labia. Her pussy gobbled up my cock with ease, and we both gasped when I slid all the way in until the bulbous head of my member smashed against her soft, spongy insides.

"Fuck me, Sk'lar. Fuck me hard."

I put my hands on either side of her hips and thrust for all I was worth. She was primed and ready, and I glided in and out of her with growing confidence. We coordinated our bodies for maximum effect as she ground herself onto me. Her cries of passion echoed off the walls of the bedroom. Sunlight caught her lovely red hair and revealed a whole spectrum of hidden colors. Right now, there was nowhere else I would rather be than conjoined with her like this.

"Oh god. I'm coming." Phryne screamed as I slapped

my thighs into hers in a rapid tattoo. My hamstrings cramped a bit, but one of my implants released an inhibitor to slow the effects of lactic acid. It was supposed to help me run longer, but if it helped me give my lover a fantastic screw, then all the better.

Phryne came, and then came again, and I found myself on the verge of release, too. But I was determined to keep this connection for a bit longer. Besides, I loved the way she sounded when she came. I wanted to make Phryne as happy as she made me.

At last, she threw her head back and howled like a predator at the full moon. I allowed myself release, and my hot seed filled her up.

Sweating, we collapsed onto the bed, me lying half on top of her. I enveloped her in my arms as she let out a contented sigh.

If this wasn't paradise, it was as close to it as I was ever likely to see.

PHRYNE

Sk'lar was horrible for my work ethic. I had stacks of reports to go over, a dozen new security protocols to design, and I had to check up on the new alpha team members. They were still in training, but I was sure Cyrus had made all of them cry at least once by now. It was best to check in periodically to make sure no psychological damage occurred in the trainees. They'd be useless on the alpha team if that happened.

Despite all that, Sk'lar was the only thing I could think about for more than three seconds at a time. Twice today, I'd caught myself staring at a wall fantasizing about what I wanted to do with Sk'lar once we were both off work for the evening. The likelihood of both of us getting off work around the same time was small, but I could dream.

"Phryne, come in." The voice in my earpiece startled me out of my fantasies.

"What's up?" I tried to sound casual but my voice came out too high.

"Please report to the mayor's office immediately."

Something had to be up. Vidia would've paged me directly or sauntered into my office if she needed me.

I hurried down the corridor to her office. A few Strike Team Two members were stationed in front of Vidia's door. As I approached, I imagined the worst.

"What's happened?"

My question was answered the moment I saw Vidia's door.

WE DEMAND BLOOD was scrawled in thick red lettering across the surface of her door.

"Who found this?" I demanded.

"General Rouhr. He called Vidia and told her to stay home. He's probably back with her by now."

Good, that was one thing I didn't have to worry about right away.

"Has the substance been tested?"

"Leena DeWitt is on her way now."

"Have all of the security footage from last night until now sent to my console. The perpetrator will have been caught on the corridor cameras."

"Yes, ma'am."

"Take photos at every angle. Has anyone opened the office door yet?"

"No, ma'am."

"Good. No one is allowed to lay a finger on this door until I say so. It could be rigged with something. Leena DeWitt has permission to take a single, light pressure swab when she arrives."

"Yes, ma'am."

"Alpha team, come in," I said into my radio.

"Alpha team," replied Ryx.

"Can you bring an x-ray scanner, a metal scanner, a heat scanner, and anything else you think might be useful in detecting a small explosive or similar motion triggered trap to the mayor's office?"

"Yes, ma'am."

I hated how much I loved this. Of course, if Vidia was in danger, it'd be a different story. However, Vidia was safe in her home with a general to guard her, which meant I got to do what I was good at and hopefully apprehend someone in the process.

The flashing of my comm unit distracted me from examining the writing on the door. I switched my earpiece from my radio to my comm unit and accepted the transmission.

"Manka."

"Hey, it's me." Vidia's voice came through.

"Is the general with you?"

"Yes, he won't let me leave the house," she sounded agitated.

"Good. Someone's made a threat against you."

"Are you absolutely sure I can't come in?"

"Did you not hear me? You're being threatened. No, you need to say where you are, with the general."

"You'll tell me as soon as it's safe for me to come in, right?" she pleaded.

"Your priorities are more out of line than I thought they were."

"That's rich coming from you," she snorted. "Promise, okay? I really need to get into the office today."

"I can send over any reports you might need."

"It's something I have to do in person," she insisted.

"Fine. I'll let you know as soon as it's safe for you to return to your office. Though I think you should take the day off."

"No can do."

Vidia disconnected our call. I stood in the corridor trying to figure out what could be so important to Vidia that a direct threat didn't dissuade her.

Ryx arrived with my equipment shortly after Leena took her sample.

"Cursory examination reveals nothing shoved under the door or in the lock," Ryx reported.

"Great. Let's run the scanners."

There was nothing giving off any unexplainable heat signatures nor did any of the other tests we ran indicate that Vidia's door had been tampered with. I ordered everyone to step back thirty feet while I opened the door.

I'd already been shot, so at this point I wasn't afraid of getting caught in an explosion.

Thankfully, nothing happened when the door swung open. Ryx and I surveyed Vidia's office together before giving it the all clear. I radioed the lab.

"Leena, what's the origin of the writing?"

"Standard paint. I think they were trying to spook us by making it look bloody," she replied. "It's safe to wipe off with a standard rag and solution."

"Thanks." I turned to a nearby Skotan. "Has the writing been photographed?"

"Yes, ma'am."

"Great. It's safe to clean it up. I'm going to look through some security footage."

As I walked back to my office, I called Vidia on her comm unit.

"If you absolutely have to, you can come back to the office. I recommend an armed escort service."

"Is that really necessary?"

"Vidia, need I remind you that we've both been shot purely because someone didn't like you? If you deliberately put yourself in danger, it'll be like I got shot for nothing."

"That was a rather sentimental observation, not at all like you," she observed.

"I've been spending more time with Sk'lar. He's softened me up."

"I can't wait to hear all about it."

She disconnected and I settled into my desk chair to sift through hours of footage.

I started with this morning's footage and rewound until the writing on the doorway disappeared.

Thankfully, the security feed didn't cut out. That would've indicated a much more advanced operation, possibly with the help of someone who already had access to the building. I wasn't in the mood to be betrayed by anyone again.

Instead, I found a scrawny individual sneaking through the corridor. They wore a black hood obscuring their features. I couldn't tell if it was a man or a woman. They wrote the message in paint and crept back out. I followed the hooded vandal through the building via the security cameras. They climbed through a first story window.

All of the windows were monitored. The vandal shouldn't have been able to get through without tipping off the system. I pulled up the logs from the window monitors that night. The window in question had a monitor that miraculously started glitching when the vandal arrived. I flipped back to the security footage looking for when the vandal originally entered. I watched him (or her) pull out a small device and press it against the window. It must've delivered some kind of electric shock that overloaded the monitor.

Great, now that had to be replaced. All of the window monitors did. Vidia was not going to be happy about that.

No thanks to me, she'd finally balanced out the budget.

It annoyed me that I couldn't identify the vandal, but I figured if they wanted to do serious damage, they would've done so. Besides, they'd exposed fatal security flaws in our system. Really, they'd done us a favor. I'd love to tell them that one day. The look on their face would be priceless.

Despite the lack of clarity on the cams, I took stills of the vandal and sent them to every department. Everyone in the building should be aware. And on the off chance that this vandal worked here, hopefully the stills would spook them. I liked to think none of the current staff was stupid enough to sneak through a building decked out with surveillance cameras.

Satisfied that I'd done all I could do for the time being, I decided to check in on Vidia. I'd been reviewing the footage for a few hours. She was bound to have arrived by now.

The newly cleaned door to her office was open. As I approached, I realized she wasn't alone in her office.

"The scans came back." I recognized Evie's voice. I paused before entering the office.

"What did you find?" Vidia sounded nervous.

"I'm not sure," replied Evie. "There are unusual patterns I've never seen before. They don't match up with any known brain disease, cancer, or mental illness."

"So, should I worry?"

"Are you still experiencing symptoms?"

"I am."

"Then I would be cautious. Pay close attention to what happens when you feel strange."

"Don't you have any theories?" Vidia snapped. Vidia never snapped.

"One. But I'd prefer not to share it until I have more evidence to back it up."

"Tell me. That's an order from your mayor."

"It could be parasitic like Fen said," Evie said slowly. "Like I said, I don't have enough data to fully corroborate this theory but, based on the brain scans, alone I've seen some organisms that leave somewhat similar signatures."

"A parasite," Vidia whispered. "Does that mean it's transferable?"

"I don't know," Evie replied softly.

"How can we find out?"

"I can run more tests."

"But parasites are still organic life forms," Vidia said. "At least I think they are. These parasites are, too?"

"I don't know," Evie said again, dejectedly.

"If it's transferrable, that means anyone could feel what I've been feeling." Vidia sounded afraid. "I'm strong enough to keep those feelings at bay, but is everyone else? We have to find out what this is before people have the chance to give into it."

"We'll figure it out, Vidia. We always do."

"We have to. The consequences are too great if we don't."

SK'LAR

The four of us sat in Rouhr's office, Rouhr, Vrehx, Karzin, and myself. We sat in his office, all of us trying to lay our fingers on the pulse of what was happening and trying to figure out a way to deal with it.

The electrical pulse generator that the humans at the compound had made and used been a prototype, or so the people that used it believed. They had created it, but a few of the people from the compound had left before they'd decided to attack Puppet Master. There was a chance that one of them knew how to make it and could potentially be making another one.

"How do we deal with the generator if they make another one?" Vrehx asked. "I mean, based on your reports, as soon as you shot it," he looked at Rouhr as he spoke, "it started to build up a charge that ended up bringing the whole tunnel system down. There's a minor sinkhole there now."

"Well, if I knew, we wouldn't be sitting here, now would we?" Rouhr countered. He held up a hand in apology. "Sorry. It's just been very stressful lately and I'm losing track of what the zet is going on. As if the rebuild of everything and the hatred of us wasn't bad enough, now we have friends suddenly turning on us, and that has me coming towards my wit's end."

Vrehx nodded in understanding. "It's okay. At least you don't have a baby keeping you awake in the middle of the night."

Rouhr chuckled. "True. How's that going, by the way?"

"Jeneva is absolutely brilliant. She's handling the little guy phenomenally. I'm still stumbling my way through things," he sighed. "I swear, I did not know how much a baby could release or how bad it would smell when they filled their diaper."

We all laughed a bit as he smiled at his own confession.

"But," he continued. "I wouldn't change a second of it. I always thought that parents who marveled at every little thing their child did were stupid and caught up in the moment, but I swear, every little thing he does is sensational."

"Welcome to parenthood, my friend," Karzin said. "I've watched as friends and family have done the exact same. Here's the thing, he's the first of his kind. How will he respond to whatever this skrell is?"

That had been something that we hadn't considered, and all of us sat there, wide-eyed, stricken, and confused.

"Rek," Vrehx swore.

"Sorry, my friend," Karzin said. "I didn't mean to ruin the moment."

"I know. It's okay. It's something I have to consider. If we aren't able to stop whatever is causing our friends to switch, I have to consider what may become of all our loved ones, not just mine." Vrehx was right. This seemed to be affecting only the humans thus far, and that could include the women that we were all with.

"Well, now that we've livened up this party, what do you all say we find a way to end it?" I said. "We're facing something that can turn our friends at any moment. We're facing a bunch of people that don't like us just through natural prejudices. We're still facing a food shortage, although that is improving. We're dealing with a creature that is literally the heart and soul of the planet, and if either of these anti-alien movements find a way to kill him, they kill everything and everyone. Oh, and we have no way to get off the planet. Does that about sum it up?"

"Aren't you the happy little reminder of all that's terrible?" Karzin said flatly. "But that seems to be about the basics of our troubles, yes."

Despite the fact that his anger issues had lessened since he found Annie, he was still hard to deal with when he was surly.

"So, how do we deal with it all?" Vrehx asked.

"Take it one problem at a time," I said. "Then, we move on to the next one."

"Sk'lar is right," General Rouhr said. "Let's line up the issues in a row, then take them down one at a time."

We all nodded.

"Okay," Rouhr said with a clap of his hands. "Food shortage. How is that coming along?"

Vrehx was the one to answer. "Better. With Puppet Master able to finally help, we're growing crops at a faster rate. They still take time, but we should be back to normal levels within a year, maybe a little longer. But we're on the right track."

"Good," the general said. "I know you're not happy playing food inventory, but I appreciate the help."

"My pleasure, sir. It keeps me close to Jeneva and the boy."

"Okay. What about the anti-alien movement? I know we have some human-only settlements popping up, but so far they've seemed peaceful enough," Rouhr told us. "But what about places like the compound we were at ten days ago? Have we found any others?"

This time, Karzin spoke up. "Not that we've been able to see. I've been using the satellites that Fen launched to try to get a sky view of everything, but either they're really good at hiding, or they're keeping themselves in the towns that are already established. So far, I haven't been able to figure out how they communicate and grow their numbers without tipping someone off and that someone coming to tell us."

"So, they have to know who is against us, or on the fence about us, already?"

Karzin nodded. "Yes. That's the only thing I can think of. I mean, how could they get more people to join them without someone sending up signals? They can't be killing them or kidnapping them, or else that would send up some serious signals on its own."

"Okay, so that's a problem that we still need to work on, yes?" Rouhr asked.

"Yes."

The general sat back in his chair and let out a slow, deep breath. "Let's move on to Puppet Master. If that generator can hurt him that badly, there has to be a way to protect him, but we don't have enough hands to do that, not with everything else happening."

"Then we let him protect himself," I said. "We have to trust him."

"Do we?" Karzin spoke up. "I'm still not fully convinced as to his role in all this."

"Hey, all living creatures want to live until they don't," I said. "I haven't seen signs of him giving up, have you?"

"No, but..."

"But nothing," I interrupted. "Puppet Master has shown us nothing but a willingness to live and to fix what was damaged by us and the Xathi. I think we need to show a little bit of trust to the one being that has already shown he can shut us all down. Or have you forgotten the dome?"

"No, I haven't. I was part of bringing it down, remember?" Karzin spat back at me.

"Yeah, I do," I answered back. "But that doesn't mean he hasn't already found a way to counter or block the poison we created. If he wanted to kill all of us, I have a feeling he could do so easily, yet he hasn't. So we trust in him and we bring him in to help. We could use his knowledge. Maybe he could reach out and probe the minds of people, find the ones that hate us and help us locate them."

"He could, but it would take too long for him to do so," Rouhr cut in. "With people he doesn't know and hasn't touched, he has to push hard to get inside their minds. It could take him hours to do so."

"Okay," I conceded. "That's not a great plan then, but it's still something. Any other ideas?"

"What about Fen and the Urai?" Karzin asked. "Have they found anything out beyond the video they showed of the rifts?"

"Nothing as of yet," Rouhr answered. "They're still looking into it, and talking with everyone they can, but we've made no headway with identifying if there's any parasites."

"Great," Karzin responded. "The smartest beings we know are arguing with one another and we still don't have a clue as to what's causing friends and loved ones to turn on us. Oh, another question. Has anyone thought about what became of the ship that brought the humans?"

"It was a drop-off," Vrehx answered. "They were delivered, then the ship left. There was supposed to be a communication array established, but apparently the first generation decided not to. They wanted to run this world free of Earth influences."

"I'm going to assume you've been doing some studying during your time off work," General Rouhr chuckled. "Even I didn't know any of this."

"Jeneva didn't either," Vrehx said back. "She was just as surprised as I was. Essentially, we're stuck here unless we can convince Thribb, and whoever is able to stay on our side, to somehow build us a new ship."

"And the likelihood of getting one built soon is slim, is that what you're saying?" I asked.

"I don't know. Maybe."

"Look," the general cut in. "We're learning some things here, but we're not going to be able to get anywhere if we argue, fight amongst ourselves, or begin to doubt things about ourselves. What we need to do is get more minds on this."

"Are you sure we can trust those minds?" Karzin asked. "I love Annie, but I'm finding myself holding things from her because I don't know if she'll suddenly turn on us. We need to make the 'switch' our priority."

"And I agree with you," Rouhr said. "I truly do. But, for right now, we need as many minds on this as we can get. The more minds, the more ideas, the more opportunities we have to figure something out."

"But," Karzin started.

"'But' nothing, Karzin," Rouhr stopped him. "This meeting is over for now. We've got nothing between the four of us that we haven't already spoken about before. We need a break. I'll call in as many of us as we can trust, or at least hope to trust, in a few days. Give everyone an opportunity to think and clear their minds. Dismissed."

With that, we were done.

EPILOGUE: PHRYNE

As difficult as it was for me to admit, I'd reached some kind of breaking point. I wasn't on the verge of collapse. I wasn't going to go insane and run off to live in the jungle or anything like that. However, the past few months had been a real kick in the ass. Day after day I had shit thrown at me with no reprieve. I used to think I could work like that indefinitely. Recent events had proved me very wrong.

Sk'lar and I hardly had time for our nightly outings to the bar anymore. If we got lucky, we could drink and chat for an hour before going back to my apartment for half-asleep sex. Sk'lar would have to get up a few hours later and I'd follow soon after. It wasn't enough time to relieve stress anymore. We simply needed more time together to decompress.

If he and I kept going at this pace with no reprieve, we'd combust. Possibly in a literal sense.

I'd only been at my desk for a minute when I had a fantastic idea. I picked up my comm unit and paged Sk'lar.

"Everything okay?" he asked.

"Yes, but I need you to get back here by five."

"Why?"

"It's a surprise. Just do it." I disconnected before he could answer. He was out at the crater site today, so if he wanted to get back in time, he'd have to leave in just a few short hours. However, if I managed what I wanted to pull off, I'd have to leave now.

"Vidia," I called her name before I entered her office, just in case I stumbled into another private conversation. I hadn't told Vidia that I'd overheard her conversation with Evie. I wanted Vidia to tell me in her own time, despite how serious it'd sounded.

"What's up?" she shouted back, sounding as chipper as ever. There hadn't been any follow up to that threat on her office door. No riots had broken out in the last forty-eight hours, either. We considered that a win. My, how our standards had fallen.

"I need to go home," I stated.

Vidia lifted her brows in surprise. She quickly swallowed the tea she'd been sipping. No doubt it was piping hot.

"Is everything all right?"

"Yes, I just would like a day off."

"Did I hear that right?" Vidia narrowed her eyes.

"Is there a better way to phrase that?"

"No, I understood the words. But the meaning must be different because they came out of your mouth. Have you ever taken a day off?"

"I took a lot of days off after the final debate."

"You didn't *take* those days off. You were in a medically induced coma for part of them and in physical therapy for the rest of them. In case you forgot, you got shot that day."

"Right," I nodded. "But I didn't work, so that's technically a day off."

"This is painful to listen to. Yes, take your day off. I won't ask questions." Vidia waved me out of her office.

I hurried home to grab a few things, then I spent the next few hours in the market district of Nyheim. I kept my hood up to hide my features from anyone who might've wanted to do me harm.

Fifteen minutes before five o'clock, I was on the roof of my apartment complex. I'd set up string lights, partially for atmospheric purposes but also because there were no other lights on the roof. Sk'lar and I would need lights for what we were going to do tonight.

I also laid out soft mats for protection and I lit a few

herb sticks so the air smelled more like the seaside and less like a dirty roof. Yes, this night was going to be perfect.

I answered my comm unit on the first tone.

"Where are you?" Sk'lar asked.

"On the roof. Come up."

Once again, I hung up on him.

A few moments later, Sk'lar clambered up the fire escape. He took in the glowing sight of the roof with a huge smile on his face.

"What's all this?" he asked.

"We've never actually been on a date," I shrugged.

"I cooked you dinner once."

"You bought dinner and then heated it up!" I exclaimed.

"I still did all of the work to make sure you were fed."

"You doing all of the work wasn't a date. It was just you being nice," I teased. "Besides, by that point, we'd already had all of our firsts."

"Firsts?"

"First kiss, having sex for the first time," I listed.

"This is uncharacteristically sentimental of you." I detected a note of suspicion in his voice.

"This is the first time I'm giving my all to a relationship that has nothing to do with work."

"We met at work," he pointed out.

"Don't ruin the moment." I stuck my tongue out at him.

"Have you been drinking?"

"Is it so hard to believe I could be ready to have fun without the influence of alcohol? Don't answer that," I said before he could say anything.

"Can I ask what your intentions are? You've got quite the romantic setup here." Sk'lar looked around at the roof again.

"Romantic? I'm not here for romance. Catch."

He turned around just in time to catch the training staff I tossed his way.

"You want to train?"

"Spar," I corrected. "You've used one before, right?"

"Of course." He tossed the staff from one hand to the other to test its weight. "I think staff training is standard on any planet."

"Then let's go," I insisted.

"Do all of your dates go like this?" he asked as our staves clashed together. I whirled to evade his strike, then drove the butt of my staff into his shoulder.

"They would if I went on dates," I replied. "But you're the first one who's ever been able to handle me."

"I'm honored." Sk'lar knocked out the back of my knee with his staff, throwing me off balance. He pinned me to the mat, effectively immobilizing me.

"Best two out of three?" I offered.

Sk'lar dipped his head to kiss me before letting me up.

"This is the first time I've beaten you at something that involves a long stick. No rematch. I'm keeping my win."

"Fine." I rolled my eyes and grinned. "I made dinner, too, if you're hungry."

"Now you're stealing my date ideas?"

"You didn't invent making dinner for someone," I countered.

"I did in this relationship."

"Say that again," I requested with a smile.

"I did in this relationship," he repeated hesitantly.

"Thank you. I just wanted to hear you say we're in a relationship."

"I wanted to be in one much sooner, but you were too skittish," Sk'lar teased.

We walked over to the wicker basket I'd brought up in advance. We sat side by side on the mats to eat the underwhelming sandwiches I'd made.

"I wasn't skittish!" I protested. "I just overthought everything."

"You can say that again," Sk'lar said between bites. "I won't hold it against you. I'm glad you took the time to think everything through before deciding what you want."

"You are?"

"Of course. That's how I know you really want me."

I scooted closer to Sk'lar and laid my head on his shoulder.

"This is much better than a one-night stand," I sighed.

"I agree." He pressed a kiss into my forehead. "Want to know a secret?"

"What?"

"I'd noticed you long before we started working together."

A blush blossomed in my cheeks.

"I noticed you the moment we all started working on the same floor. Your dedication and competence stood out from everyone else."

"Most women like it when you tell them they're prettier than the others." I bumped his shoulder.

"You're not most women."

"I noticed you, too," I offered.

"I find that hard to believe."

"We interacted a number of times before we worked together. I never learned your name and I didn't recognize you instantly each time, but I knew who you were."

"This is the strangest romantic conversation between two beings."

"You're an alien and I'm an orphan. What do you expect?"

Sk'lar tipped his head back and laughed.

"What did you think when you noticed me?" he asked.

"You were one of the few who didn't instantly annoy me," I said. "You didn't mince words. You gave direction and took direction efficiently. You didn't make stupid mistakes and you didn't stretch beyond your abilities, which are extensive, by the way. I knew you were talented at your job, too."

"Yet my name and my face escaped you?"

"Vidia says I have to realign my priorities," I sniffed.

"I think your priorities are perfect. She's lucky to have you on her team."

"I'm lucky to have you on mine."

Sk'lar bent his head to kiss me. I let thoughts of anything other than him drift away and disappear like smoke. Those thoughts would return sooner rather than later, but right now I just wanted to be with him.

"Whatever happens," he murmured when we broke apart, "I'm grateful that we'll be doing this together."

"Together," I repeated.

We stayed on the roof for a long time watching both the stars above us and the city below us. Looking down on all the people, I could convince myself that the rest of the planet took a night off, too. Everyone would find peace tonight. Even if it was just one night, it counted for so much more than that.

LETTER FROM ELIN

Whoo hoo! This begins the what I think of as the third season of Conquered World. It's a crazy sort of magic to imagine a story line that spreads and braids back on itself, and then bring it to life and share it with people.

Thank you so much for being part of that magic.

Next up, for more questions and answers - Jalok!

Keep reading for a sneak peek.

XOXO,

Elin

JALOK: SNEAK PEEK

Dottie

I woke up with the rising sun as I had the day before. I'd spent the majority of the last two weeks in a windowless lab inputting data that, ultimately, made no sense to our computers. I worked out of Kaster, my home city. When I first took this contract with General Rouhr and his scientists, they wanted me to move to Nyhiem to work. I declined.

When bad things happened, they happened in Nyhiem first. The anti-alien radicals had a huge foothold in that city. Not long ago, there'd been a shooting that nearly killed the mayor of Nyhiem and her personal bodyguard or something like that.

No way was I about to relocate to such a dangerous place.

Besides, I loved Kaster. My family lived there since the city was first founded. The Xathi did a number on it which was all the more reason or me not to leave. When I wasn't working, I volunteered with different relief organizations within the city. The school was still in shambles. The kids of Kaster were learning out of a tent surrounded by rubble. The teachers were working for free for now. If I wasn't on the job now, I'd be there.

The sunlit stretch of the tent above me did nothing to stop the brightness of the morning sun from creeping in. That's how I liked it. I was a sunlight creature. Cloudy days put me in a bad mood. Back home, the running joke was that I was secretly part plant and that's why I became an environmental scientist.

I stepped out of my tent to bask in the morning rays. I arrived here yesterday, too late in the evening to warrant setting up my equipment. My tent was set up on the edge of the crater left behind by the explosion of the alien ship, Vengeance. Aside from some unidentifiable chunks of metal strewn about, there was nothing left of the ship that crash landed here so many months ago.

Shame. I would've liked to see that.

Recently, the crater was attacked by a group of anti-alien radicals not long ago. They targeted the sentient vines of the Puppet Master. The exposed vines were singed and slashed. Today, I planned to take samples from the wounds to see what the radicals used.

This was my first time back here in about two weeks. The Puppet Master was attacked last week. While I was glad I wasn't here during the attack, I felt terrible for not being there to defend the Puppet Master.

When this job was first offered to me, I accepted without thinking much on it. The salary alone was worth doing whatever it was they wanted me to do. On top of that, I'd been studying plants and their effect on their environments for nearly seven years. Taking this job was a no brainer.

Then I was taken out to the far deserts, beyond the borders of the settled lands. General Rouhr and a few human scientists took me down into a massive crater. When they presented me to the plant they wanted me to study, I nearly fainted.

Of course, I'd learn that plant wasn't at all the correct term for the Puppet Master.

When he first spoke to me, I was terrified. I'd never felt anything whisper directly into my brain like that before. It felt like an invasion.

I almost quit the job right then and there. The money was too good, though. Not to mention that I spent half my life becoming an expert in my field. If they'd approached my lab with this offer a few months ago, the job would've gone to my boss Dr. Miles Crane. Unfortunately, Miles wasn't with us anymore. He wasn't killed during the Xathi invasion like many were. No, he suffered a far worse fate.

When Xathi hybridism spread to the outlying cities, the men in Kaster were quick to act. Most of the men in Kaster were burly fisherman types who were comfortable battling raging storms in little boats. General Rouhr offered several of Kaster's man positions in his ranks. A few went. Most of declined. Kaster was a small city, more of a town. The community was close-knit. We were all family.

When the Kaster men rounded up anyone showing signs of hybridism, Miles Crane was among them. His case progressed rapidly. Within a day, he'd completely lost himself. I wasn't there when he was killed. I couldn't bear it.

I was his right hand so when General Rouhr requested an environmental scientist, the job offer fell to me. The kind of money General Rouhr and his people were willing to pay was enough to fix up the school and buy new stalls for the open market.

So, I toughed up and started talking with the Puppet Master. He was intelligent, naturally. I was expecting that once I knew he could speak into my mind. I didn't expect him to be kind. He was willing to help the humans and the aliens rebuild the planet.

My job was to figure out how the Puppet Master worked, so to speak. The Puppet Master described himself as the beating heart of the planet. I wanted to know how that was possible.

My first few meetings with the Puppet Master consisted of him demonstrating his abilities for me. I watched in awe as he sprouted flowers and soothed irate forest creatures. In those sessions of observation, I realized what an extraordinary creature I'd been given the opportunity to work with. I started staying down in the crater with the Puppet Master long after observation sessions finished.

I told the Puppet Master about my home and my family. He told me of his species and how long it's been since he sensed others of his kind. I invited him for dinner next time I was with my family again. That seemed to amuse him.

I'd go as far as to call us friends now. More than once I've found myself climbing into his crater in the middle of the night to talk about a bad dream I had or a fear that nagged me. The Puppet Master listened with great patience. Even if he couldn't relate to my feelings, he always tried to help.

I spent the last two weeks back in Kaster analyzing what I could at the lab within the city. Anything beyond my means was sent to the lab in Nyhiem. I had three datapads filled with analyses from Nyhiem I planned to spend my nights interpreting. Right now, I wanted to speak to the Puppet Master.

In the interest of preserving infrastructure within the cities, the Puppet Master wasn't allowed to spread his tendrils too close to city limits. Otherwise, I would just ask him to extend a vine through the Kaster lab window and do all of my interviews there.

A hole had been blown in the northeast side of the crater making a tunnel. I walked across the expanse of the crater and through the mouth of the tunnel. Thick vines lined the cavern walls. The deeper into the earth I went, the fewer injuries I saw on the Puppet Master's vines.

When I found a location free of injuries, I placed my hand against a cool, firm vine.

"Welcome, Dottie," came the layered voice of the Puppet Master in my head. *"I predicted you'd be deployed here."*

"How are you?" I asked. "Are you in any pain?"

"Some but I will soon heal."

"How do you heal?" I took out my recorder. Since the Puppet Master's voice was purely telepathic, I couldn't record him directly. I planned on repeating everything he said to me out loud.

"I generate my own healing enzymes that can repair

wounds," he explained. *"Don't be too impressed. You do the same thing when you're injured."*

I laughed as I repeated his answer.

"At the core of all things, I am a lifeform just as you are despite the fact that I am what you would call ancient," he continued. *"Pay close enough attention and you will find we have more similarities than we do differences."*

That's why I loved talking to the Puppet Master. He had the ability to make me feel so small yet so significant at the same time.

"We refer to you as male," I prompted. "Does that mean there are females too?"

"Male and female refers to reproductive capabilities. My species does not reproduce. We are eternal."

"Then where did you come from?"

"That even I can't tell you," he said. *"One instant I was not. The next instant I was. In the history of this universe, I am but a youngling in the footsteps of those that came before me. While I may have knowledge over my eons of existence, I have but scratched the surface of our reality."*

"You're a mystery." I affectionately patted the vines. "I like solving mysteries."

"I will tell you what I know though I can't promise your limited brain will be able to comprehend it," he said.

"Hey!"

"That was not meant to be insulting. It is simply true."

"I know."

"You're very intelligent for a human." A thin tendril reached out to wrap around my wrist. It was the Puppet Master's equivalent of a pat on the shoulder.

"You're lucky I like you so much," I teased. "Let's move back to your healing abilities. Do they extend to only your own body or the rest of the planet?"

"The rest of the planet is my body. I am simply the heart and the mind."

"I know but I need a way to measure that," I chuckled.

"Some things are incapable of being measured in a lab."

"Don't start getting philosophical on me."

"We are all philosophy, child." I liked explaining new things to the Puppet Master. It made me feel less useless.

"Long ago back on Earth a bunch of guys sat around and asked questions that appeared to have simple answers but were really far more complicated than originally anticipated. Even with all of our advancements, we still can't answer most of them."

"Such as?"

"My favorite has always been what is the true reality? If a group of people simultaneously witness the same event, each has a slightly different perception. Which one is the true one?"

"Excellent," the Puppet Master hummed.

"What is?"

"The answer you seek is found in the question itself."

And that's how I learned the Puppet Master enjoyed philosophy.

Jalok

Toe to heel, Cazak and I crept up on our unwary prey. Looming, half rebuilt buildings hemmed us in on either side, making our task all the more dangerous.

The two of us were supposed to be on patrol, checking for any glaring structural issues and making sure the anti-alienists weren't lurking about Nyheim proper. Ever since the unrest during the election and the attack on the Puppet Master, command was extra paranoid about even the slightest problem. All three Strike teams found themselves utilized for even routine patrols such as the one we were sent upon that day.

"Do you see it?" Cazak spoke in a low tone, because a whisper can carry much further in the dark than one would suspect. I squinted, peering in the gloom, until I saw a flash of light behind a rubbish bin. A spindly leg splayed out as a deer-like creature rooted about for scraps.

"Yeah. It's a tiny one."

"Even small ones can be a threat, especially to a civilian."

Grunting, I drew my side arm. The sleek pistol had been painted unreflective black, making it perfect for urban stealth ops. It seems like overkill for such a tiny, delicate seeming creature. Luurizi, however, could be known as vicious creatures that could easily kill a human. Or even a Valorni. The little shits would charge at damn near anything, and their feet were so sharp they could pierce all but the highest grade armor plating.

Even my innate sheath of scales wouldn't prove sufficient against its attack. I deployed them anyway, because sometimes the hollow rail gun rounds could ricochet after impact. Cazak grinned, flexing his own scales into view but he still ducked behind the corner of a building for cover.

"Coward," I spoke in a low voice as I creep up for a better shot.

"Don't talk to me that way. Who was it who recommended your transfer from the Ground Team to Strike Team Three? Show some gratitude."

"Yeah, thanks for getting me this sweet gig where I kill fairytale creatures in the most gruesome manner possible. In the dark. In the middle of the night—"

"Are you going to talk it to death?"

"You've been trying to do that to me for years."

The Luurizi's head popped up, focusing its gaze in our direction. Our voices had grown louder during the exchange, it seemed. With a shrill cry akin to broken glass, it galloped across the pavement.

"Now look at what you've done."

I didn't have time for a retort. The Luurizi loped ever faster, then drove its forelegs into the ground. Its back legs gathered together with the front, and then it bunched up its body and sprang, all in the matter of a split second.

My gaze tracked its flight, and I aimed my pistol for its midsection. One squeeze of the trigger, and the creature exploded in midair, showering me with bits of bone and gooey tissue.

"Srell." Wiping myself clean, I staggered back onto the main thoroughfare while Cazak laughed hysterically.

"Come on, hero. Patrol's over. Let's go grab some beverages."

Grumbling, I fell into step beside him. We headed toward the towering buildings of the city proper, where the damage had already been largely repaired.

"Things sure have been crazy lately."

I glanced over at Cazak, and noted his worried frown.

"Yes, it's been hectic for a while, and I don't see it calming down anytime soon."

"This is a strange place to be a Skotan. Cooperating with other races instead of dominating them."

The words bubbled out of my mouth before I could really consider them.

"Do you ever think we'll find a way to get back home?"

"We're going to stop at the pub first, I told you—"

"No, I mean, the homeworld."

Cazak's jaw worked silently, and I could feel the longing from him as well.

"I don't know. Maybe they can figure out a way to open a rift to get us home, someday."

"If we're allowed to use rifts again."

"True."

We walked in silence, our destination locked in for the recreational district. There we would find a pub friendly to us soldier types, where you can be around other people who got it, even if they weren't Skotan. Cazak and I ordered some drinks and sat down at a booth. I barely tasted my drink, and I doubt he enjoyed his own much more.

"I'd like to go home, someday."

Cazak looked over at me and shrugged as if it doesn't matter, though I knew it did.

"What's the matter, don't like this place?"

"Well, it's not that. I'm certainly not a xenophobe like the anti-alienists. It's just that—on the homeworld, we belonged. Here, we'll never really fit in. Or at least, that's' what it feels like."

"If you were back home, you would probably be on a ship fighting the Xathi."

"That's where I *want* to be." I took a long pull from the bottle, and set the half empty vessel down. "I belong in battle, fighting an enemy I can see, not having to worry about pissing off a giant space lettuce or having some invisible non corporeal being root around in my brain and make me a meat suit."

"The Xathi are terrifying, Jalok. Worse than any of that, if you ask me."

"Well, I didn't ask you, did I? Fighting is what I do. Soldiering is what I was made for. Cooling my heels on this planet while our brothers and sisters die fighting those damn bugs is torture."

"Look at it this way." Rokul spread his hands out, as if encompassing the galaxy between them. "They're at home, fighting for the good of Skotans everywhere, and we're here, fighting for the good of Skotans—and humans and K'ver and all the rest. You can't be everywhere at once. But you can make a difference right here."

"Yeah, but we're not supposed to be here. That's all I'm saying. Everything is wrong about this planet. The others might love it, but Skotan are supposed to spend most of our time in high gravity."

"Yes, but that makes us stronger here, and gives us greater mass."

"That's true, but our hearts evolved to beat against a much stronger G force. I was reading a briefing from the science office about concerns that our hearts might beat too quickly and lead to a risk of cardiovascular disease."

Rokul snorted, and flashed an uncaring glare my way.

"You think too much. Look at you, you're a freaking walking tank and you want to read science reports? You should be balancing a sweet scaly thing on each one of those massive guns when you hit the sack tonight. Instead you want to act like a galaxy class nebbish."

"I find science interesting. What else am I supposed to do to pass my off time?"

"Drinking and screwing, you ignoramus. You're with Strike Team Three now. We're the best of the best of the best!"

He slapped me hard on my shoulder, and I let the matter drop.

We trudged on for a time without speaking. At length Cazak glanced over and punched me on the arm.

"Hey, if you want to feel less homesick, you could practice the traditional songs."

"There's so little time. Besides, Skotan ballads were meant to be sung on the Skotan homeworld. They just don't sound the same any place else."

That ended the debate, for now. All I knew at the time was, while many of our new allies are good people, I just wanted to go back where I belonged.

Dottie

"We have a big day ahead of us today," I announced as I settled into a comfortable sitting position inside the tunnel.

"You say that every time," the Puppet Master replied telepathically.

"Because it's true every time," I countered.

Sitting on the dirt with my back against one of the Puppet Master's vines, I started setting up my equipment. I carefully attached tiny neuro-monitors to the flesh of the vine.

"Did that hurt?"

"Did what hurt?" The Puppet Master replied.

"Never mind."

My equipment was acceptable, but it wasn't top of the line. I only got the top of the line stuff if I checked it out from the Nyhiem lab. I knew that some of the aliens traveled through what were essentially portals but that method of travel wasn't available to the average scientist yet. If I wanted to go to Nyhiem, I'd have to go the old-fashioned way. That wasn't something I wanted to do. It'd cut into my time with the Puppet Master

"A wise choice," the Puppet Master whispered to my consciousness.

"You can read my thoughts even if I'm not attempting to directly commune with you?"

"You've made physical contact once." A tendril tapped me on the shoulder and pointed to the vine I leaned up against. *"Once direct contact is made, a link between our minds is forged forever. As long as you are in my vicinity, I'm listening and can reply."*

"Is that how you commune with the living trees?" I asked.

"No," he sighed. *"They don't possess enough sentience to forge a stable connection."*

"Then how did you direct them a few months ago?"

"I," the Puppet Master started to explain, then halted. *"I do not know how to answer that. It is similar to if I*

asked you how you breathe or how you think. I perform the action without thought."

"Interesting." I tapped my chin with a stylus. "I have an idea."

"What's that?"

"We're going to do an experiment."

I pushed myself up from the ground and brushed the dirt off the seat of my pants. Motioning for the Puppet Master to follow me, in whatever way he was capable of doing so, I walked out of the tunnel. The earth around my feet shifted as I walked as the Puppet Master's vines extended out.

I climbed out of the crater. Halfway up, I lost my footing. It wasn't a far fall but the Puppet Master burrowed up vines to catch me anyway.

"Thanks." I gave the vine a pat.

Once out of the crater, I walked through a copse of trees into the forest. Since the Xathi invasion, creature populations dropped considerably. Walking through the forest was a death wish before. Now, it was just highly unrecommended.

I stopped in a small clearing. Thanks to the Puppet Master and the efforts of dedicated citizens, the forest had grown back. It wasn't what it used to be. I could still see chunks of sky through the canopy and most of the trees still had tinges of brown death on their trunks. It was progress, though. The forest would be in top shape in no time.

The Puppet Master's vines rose out of the earth beside me. I reached out and pressed my palm against one.

"It's my duty to advise you that being here is unwise," the Puppet Master warned.

"Why? I have the ultimate protection." I gave the vines another pat.

"What sort of experiment are you trying to perform?"

"I'm going to attract one of the sentient trees. You're going to stop it from attacking me. While you do that, you're going to tell me everything you're thinking and feeling."

"Thinking is an inaccurate term for what I do."

"I know but I'm human, remember? Limited understanding of beings and brains bigger than my own. Now, will you do this?"

The Puppet Master went silent for a few moments.

"A Durindium is already on your scent," he stated.

"A what?"

Before the Puppet Master could respond, a creature leaped down from the canopy above. Its body was long, lean, and feline in proportions. Sharp obsidian talons dug into the earth as it landed. Its face looked avian with a sharp, bony beak. Around its neck was a fan of growths that looked like thick flower petals. It reminded me of a lion's mane

It eyed me with its split pupil stare and let out a shriek that made my ears ring.

"Find a way to stop it from attacking me." My voice shook as I spoke.

"Its willpower is substantial," the Puppet Master replied.

The Durindium slowly circled me. I pivoted, keeping my body square with its body. It was looking for a weak point, a good place to pounce.

"Is willpower a key factor in determining how you control another creature?" I kept my voice steady. Focusing on the experiment would help keep my fear under control. I had a feeling the Durindium could smell fear.

"Yes. Right now, I'm negotiating with the Durindium's essence, it's soul if you will," he explained.

The Durindium snapped it's beak and hissed.

"It doesn't look like it's going well."

"It's not."

"Why would you tell me that," I whimpered.

The Durindium swiveled to face me head on. It lowered its haunches in preparation to spring forward right at me.

"Now would be a good time to wrap up negotiations," I pleaded.

The Puppet Master didn't answer.

A wave of doubt washed over me. What if the Puppet Master wasn't my friend at all? What if he was still an enemy of the humans at heart?

The Durindium leaped forward. I closed my eyes and curled myself downward as if that would protect me from its slashing talons. I heard it's feet land on the forest floor but no impact came. It's hot breath whipped through my hair.

Against my better judgment, I looked up. I was face to face with the Durindium, my nose less than an inch from its protruding beak.

I raised a shaking hand and touched the Puppet Master's vines.

"So," I gulped. "The negotiations went well?"

"I convinced the creature that eating you will bring on my wrath," the Puppet Master supplied.

Guilt hit me. I shouldn't have doubted him.

"Can you walk me through your process? I was too busy being terrified the first time."

"Certainly."

The Puppet Master must've done something to the Durindium because it suddenly let out a yelp and darted back into the forest. I released the breath I didn't realize I'd been holding.

At the Puppet Master's insistence, I agreed to go back to the safety of the crater. Once I was seated with my equipment once more, the Puppet Master began his explanation.

"What occurs between myself and another lifeform cannot be accurately put into your human vernacular," he started. *"However, I'll do my best. My lifeforce pulses through this planet like a network of rivers. All lifeforms on this planet drink from my rivers. Parts of me are parts of them. Do you understand?"*

"I do." I recorded a few notes in my field datapad and nodded for the Puppet Master to keep going.

"I control my lifeforce, even the parts that are in other lifeforms. My lifeforce becomes their lifeforce. When I take control of another creature, I'm simply taking control of my own life force."

"Why was is harder to control the Durindium than it is to control the sentient trees?" I asked.

"The Durindium is an active hunter, a strategist. Its intelligence is greater than that of the sentient trees. It's clever enough to detect an outside force in its mind and fight against it. The one that attacked you was also desperate. Its natural prey populations are far too small."

"I understand." I took down more notes. "Could you've used vines to directly manipulate the Durindium?"

"If I'd planted one of my seeds within the Durindium, I could have. However, it's more likely that would've killed the Durindium. The sentient trees make excellent hosts since

they are closer to plants than animals. They are infinitely simpler than creatures like the Durindium, who are more like animals than plants."

"Is that why you can't control humans or aliens?"

"I never said I can't control them. If I were to try, it would take a great deal of energy and it would be a lengthy battle for control. You humans and your alien friends have my lifeforce within you. You take it in every time you eat a plant or an animal from the forest."

"I appreciate that you've never tried to take over my brain," I chuckled.

"Brain is inaccurate," the Puppet Master corrected. *"But since I can't draw a more apt parallel, you're welcome for not taking over your brain."*

With a laugh, I checked the neuro-monitors I hooked up before. The monitors recorded great spikes of energy during the time of my ill-planned experiment. My field equipment couldn't fully analyze the spikes so I send them over to my lab back in Kaster. If I couldn't complete a satisfactory analysis there, I'd have to send it to the lab in Nyhiem.

"If a creature came from somewhere else, but took in your life force, would you be able to exert control over it?" I asked.

"Yes, with one exception."

"Which is?"

"My race doesn't have a proper name for them. Millennia

ago, when there were more of us and we were able to communicate, we called them the Ancient Enemies. They were older than us, more powerful than us, and capable of siphoning out lifeforce until there was nothing left."

"How awful." I made note of this new, unsettling information. "What else can you tell me about them?"

"Nothing." The Puppet Master sounded mournful. *"That's all I know. My race never learned how to combat them. We never discovered where they were from or what their purpose was, other than stealing our lives."*

"Is that something we should be worried about?"

"They haven't been active for thousands of years. I suspect they've moved on to a more plentiful galaxy."

I entered this new information into my notes. Somehow, the Puppet Master's words didn't bring me comfort.

GET *JALOK* NOW!

HTTPS://ELINWYNBOOKS.COM/CONQUERED-WORLD-ALIEN-ROMANCE/

PLEASE DON'T FORGET TO LEAVE A REVIEW!

Readers rely on your opinions, and your review can help others decide on what books they read. Make sure your opinion is heard and leave a review where you purchased this book!

Don't miss a new release! You can sign up for release alerts at both Amazon and Bookbub:

bookbub.com/authors/elin-wyn

amazon.com/author/elinwyn

For a free short story, opportunities for advance review copies, release news and the occasional cat picture, please join the newsletter!

https://elinwynbooks.com/newsletter-signup/

And don't forget the Facebook group, where I post sneak peeks of chapters and covers!

https://www.facebook.com/groups/ElinWyn/

DON'T MISS THE STAR BREED!

Given: Star Breed Book One

When a renegade thief and a genetically enhanced mercenary collide, space gets a whole lot hotter!

Thief Kara Shimsi has learned three lessons well - keep her head down, her fingers light, and her tithes to the syndicate paid on time.

But now a failed heist has earned her a death sentence - a one-way ticket to the toxic Waste outside the dome. Her only chance is a deal with the syndicate's most ruthless enforcer, a wolfish mountain of genetically-modified muscle named Davien.

The thought makes her body tingle with dread-or is it heat?

Mercenary Davien has one focus: do whatever is necessary to get the credits to get off this backwater mining colony and back into space. The last thing he wants is a smart-mouthed thief - even if she does have the clue he needs to hunt down whoever attacked the floating lab he and his created brothers called home.

Caring is a liability. Desire is a commodity. And love could get you killed.

https://elinwynbooks.com/star-breed/

ABOUT THE AUTHOR

I love old movies – *To Catch a Thief, Notorious, All About Eve* — and anything with Katherine Hepburn in it. Clever, elegant people doing clever, elegant things.

I'm a hopeless romantic.

And I love science fiction and the promise of space.

So it makes perfect sense to me to try to merge all of those loves into a new science fiction world, where dashing heroes and lovely ladies have adventures, get into trouble, and find their true love in the stars!

www.ingramcontent.com/pod-product-compliance
Lightning Source LLC
Chambersburg PA
CBHW070735180626
46818CB00007B/2863